Pirate Tales

E.W. Farnsworth

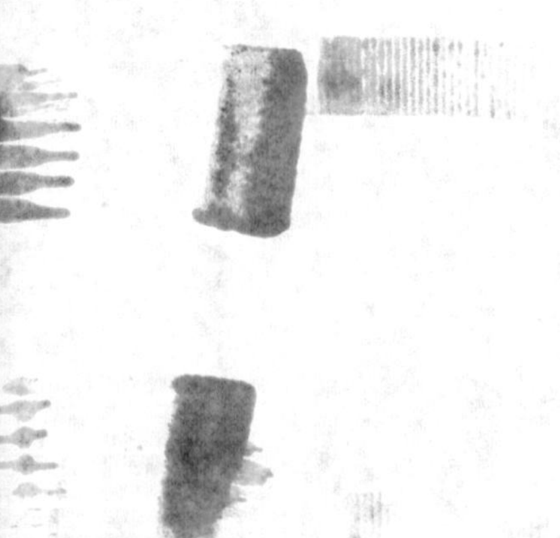

Pirate Tales

E.W. Farnsworth

ZIMBELL HOUSE
PUBLISHING, LLC
Union Lake, MI
2015

For permission requests, write to the publisher at the address below:
Attention: Permissions Coordinator
Zimbell House Publishing, LLC
PO Box 1172
Union Lake, Michigan 48387
emailto: info@zimbellhousepublishing.com

© 2016 E.W. Farnsworth
Cover Design by The Book Planners
www.TheBookPlanners.com

Published in the United States by Zimbell House Publishing, LLC
http://www.ZimbellHousePublishing.com
All Rights Reserved

Print ISBN: 978-1-942818-63-2
Kindle ISBN: 978-1-942818-64-9
Digital ISBN: 978-1-942818-65-6
Trade Paper ISBN: 978-1-945967-33-7
Library of Congress Control Number: 2016931829

First Edition: March/2016
10 9 8 7 6 5 4

Dedication

For Nadine

Acknowledgements

The following three stories were first published as individual stories in *Bottle of Rum: An Anthology of Pirate Fantasy Stories*, Full Moon Books from Horrified Press in the United Kingdom in 2016. Permission to reprint them in this collection was graciously granted on November 17, 2015 by Nathan J.D.L. Rowark, Editor.

"Pirates of Hatteras"
"Pirates of the Bermudas"
"Pirates of San Juan"

The following five stories were first published together as the novella *Pirate Tales* in *The Adventures of Pirates Anthology* of Zimbell House Publishing in 2015. Permission to republish the stories in this collection was graciously granted by Evelyn M. Zimmer, Publisher.

"Pirates of Madagascar"
"Pirates of Zanzibar"
"Pirates of Arabia"
"Pirates of the Andamans"
"Pirates of Tierra del Fuego"

Contents

E.W. Farnsworth

Reading Group Guide

A Note from the Publisher

Chapter One

Pirates of San Juan

The Sweet Cutlass struck the black skull and crossbones flag and raised the ensign of France to set anchor off San Juan after twenty-one days of successful marauding throughout the Caribbean. We were all frankly sick of being at sea, flush with bags of gold and silver coins and ready to party hard ashore in San Juan. The Captain, the Second Mate and I, left the Third Mate in charge of the ship with our hearties, cast off in the whale boat and rowed towards the port steps for a day of carousing and seeking intelligence in the bars and whore houses of the city. We planned to take each establishment as if we were climbing aboard one of our target ships with two swords and two pistols in our belts.

The first establishment we visited, the Captain's favorite, was full of merchant seamen who made way for us because they knew our type. The smell of our bodies repulsed them, but they feared for their lives when they saw our fierce demeanors, our vicious scars and our loud, colorful curses.

"A bottle of rum for each man," the Captain ordered with a scowl at the barkeep. "Drinks all around for the rest. Put everything on my tab. Make it snappy."

The barkeep hesitated for a moment too long, so the Captain drew one of his swords and, walking right up to the bar, put the sharp pointed end of his sword next to the barkeep's windpipe. That set the barkeep, his wife and his daughter in motion grabbing bottles with alacrity, and we pressed towards a table at the back of the saloon. The barkeep's wife and daughter came a few minutes later to inquire whether we needed anything in particular. So with a wink and the wild look he sometimes got around women, the Captain left me in charge of our table and went up the stairs with his two bottles of rum, his arms around the mother and daughter, singing an old bawdy sailors' song about women and the sea. The women seemed terrified of him and fearful for their lives if they should refuse him, yet they were resigned as if they had been through this before.

The Second Mate and I had no idea how long the Captain would be about his business, so we got down to serious drinking while we discussed our ship's swashbuckling exploits over the last three weeks. I was in the middle of recapping our having the entire crew of a merchantman walk the plank naked while sharks swirled below. Excited and laughing at the memory of tormenting the merchantmen, I was taking a quaff of rum at every other sentence and leering to keep my hearties' attention. At the moment I got to the punch line, the door to the bar flew open and the apparent lawmen of the town entered, armed to the teeth with swords, knives, pistols, rifles and blunderbusses. The merchantmen in the bar parted so that nothing lay between the five newcomers at the door and us at our table.

I had to think fast. "Barkeep, the Captain said that everyone should have a round on his tab, so make sure our new guests are served quickly at the bar. Everyone else should step up for seconds!"

As the stampede of customers closed in the run on the bar, the Second Mate said, "Good thinking, Abe! Now let's make for the back entrance."

"Not so fast, Rafe. If they've come for us through the front door, armed men will be waiting at the back door too." I cocked my pistols and gestured for Rafe to do the same. "Sit tight, and when I signal, take out two of our friends and we'll shift to swords."

We sat ready while the five armed lawmen pushed their way towards us through the throng. Their leader stuck his head towards me, and I recognized Sal Coinder, a former member of our pirate crew. I told the Second Mate to stand down, and I rose to embrace Sal heartily while my dagger felt for his kidney.

"Sal," I said, "It must have been seven months since we last met. You and your men, come drink with us and catch us up on the news."

Sal thought better of resisting my dagger, so he shook his head and signaled his men to drag together chairs so they could surround our table. The barkeep rushed up with a bottle of rum for each man, and he asked me sotto voce whether I had any message for the Captain. I whispered to the barkeep, "Tell him to climb out the window and meet us at the whaleboat ASAP." While the barkeep hurried up the stairs to deliver my message to the Captain, I led our table in singing a familiar song about the problems for sailors while drinking ashore. This song required a stiff drink after every stanza, and I knew all twenty stanzas by heart. When I finished the song, I started it again, but no one noticed and everyone kept right on drinking. I signaled Rafe that it was time for us to go.

"Rafe and I are going to get to the bar to fetch more rum since we're fresh out. Sal, you keep right on singing since you know the song."

The Second Mate and I pressed through the crowd to the door and entered the street, where we noticed that no noises from inside could be heard. We began trotting towards the landing. We were almost there when we heard reports of shots from the rear, so we ran to our boat and jumped in. Rafe took the oars, and I took charge of his two pistols while I scanned the shore for signs of the Captain. Rafe started laughing. The five lawmen were drunkenly winding their ways towards the whaleboat, signaling that we should stop and wait for them.

Waving one arm with a large object in the other, Sal called out, "Wait for us. We're coming with you! And we have rum." Four men raised their bottles of rum and Sal gestured to the keg he was carrying.

I told Rafe to keep on his guard for tricks. As Sal approached, I leveled my cocked pistols at him and said, "Sal, I'll cut you down where you stand if you can't explain what you mean."

Sal stuttered, "Don't shoot. Me and my mates are all pirates looking to ship aboard the Sweet Cutlass for a normal share. Landlubber living—faugh—you can take it. You need experienced, able-bodied seamen who know how to board and fight. So sign us up."

I was skeptical. Free rum or not, this was too sudden for me to lower my guard. For all I knew, this could easily be a sly trap. "Sal, you and all your mates put your weapons on the ground in front of you and step back two paces. Good. Now, Sal, you come forward so we can talk terms."

"Abe, I'm serious about our shipping aboard. I take it you are First Mate now, so you can make the decision."

"The Captain makes all decisions for the Sweet Cutlass. You know that. Just now I can't locate the Captain, so we'll have to wait for him." As if on cue, the Captain appeared at the second-story window of the public house and lowered tied sheets, by which he climbed down to the street level. He adjusted his tricorn and arranged his swords so that he could walk, turned and blew kisses to the two women who came to the window to see him off, and he marched in stately fashion to where Sal and I had faced off.

"Well, if it isn't Sal, the mystery pirate, looking much too civilized for our company." The Captain said this with a look of mild amusement on his face.

"Captain, like I was telling Abe, my mates and me want to ship aboard the Sweet Cutlass at an even share just like old times."

The Captain took this information in and pretended to consider the option seriously. He looked at me, and I only shrugged to indicate that I had no dog in the fight—the decision was his alone.

"Sal, you left my crew without my leave seven or eight months ago. By rights I should have you shot or taken your prisoner and keel-hauled at sea. I do, however, need men to replace a few unfortunates who were lost when we took our last merchantman. If we had to shanghai a crew, we wouldn't know their mettle. I do know yours, you skunk. This is my first and last offer to all of you; ship aboard the Sweet Cutlass at one half the normal pirate share. If you incite mutiny or decide to go AWOL again, I will make you walk the plank naked over a sea of sharks. What do you say?"

Sal did not need to consider the offer for a second. "Captain, we have a deal. May my men pick up their weapons now and ship aboard the whaleboat?"

"Not so fast, Sal," the Captain replied. "You have rum, so busy yourself drinking where you stand. Abe, Rafe and I are going out to the ship. You—Abe and Rafe—pick up the weapons of these men and put them in the whaleboat right now. If any man moves while you're doing that, he dies." With the weapons aboard the whaleboat, Rafe cast off its lines, shoved off and made headway towards the Sweet Cutlass. That left me covering the five unarmed men.

"Abe, do you want to join us drinking this rum? In this heat you've gotta be thirsty." Without waiting for a response, he leaned forward and jumped straight to the gossip. "So I heard the Captain is the real father of the barkeep's daughter and that's why he always stops at the public for drinks."

I was irritated and offended at the sailor's innuendo. "Sal, the strangest rumors go for truths on land. What the Captain does or doesn't do ashore is no concern of mine."

"Did anyone look around for the barkeep's son?"

"Why're you asking?"

"The barkeep sent him to the fort when the Captain walked into the bar. The boy was on his way there when he ran into us, and he told us to come right away to the bar. That's why we came when we did. A good thing he happened to find us before he got to the fort, ain't it?"

"This has nothing to do with the deal the Captain has cut with you. That deal is done, so live with it." I looked the man over with unmasked disdain. I could not stand the sight of him.

"Abe, these days're tough on pirates like us. You don't know who to trust anymore. Those merchantmen in the bar are from those two sloops you see at anchor. They'll be drinking all afternoon. In that time we could board both ships, take what's worth anything and scuttle the pair at anchor."

"Make the pitch to the Captain when you're aboard the Sweet Cutlass. He'll decide."

Sal nodded and looked from side to side. Then he winked like someone in the know. "And a dreadnought is headed here full sail looking for the Sweet Cutlass. That information should be worth something."

"So when does the military ship arrive?"

"Evening they'll anchor out and make for the public just like you did."

"Which direction're they coming from?"

"North, and the longer the Sweet Cutlass stays in port, the greater the danger. They aim to kill or capture and hang everyone on the Sweet Cutlass by order of the US government."

I was interested in this intelligence because we could use it, but I could not let this show. "Sal, I'm always amazed at the stories you spin. We'll see what the Captain has to say when you tell him the details."

So the five men drank rum while I watched their every move. I didn't know what the Captain was doing, but I knew he must be doing something. He was surely taking his sweet time getting the whaleboat out here to pick us up. I looked out occasionally to see the Sweet Cutlass, and I noticed that preparations were being made to get her underway. The signs were unmistakable.

Sal saw the signs too. "Abe, it appears the Sweet Cutlass will be leaving without any of us—including you. How does it feel to be marooned? I was marooned once on an island. I survived for five weeks until a passenger ship happened by to rescue me. That was no fun. At least you'll have us to keep you company." The man was jeering at me. My blood boiled, but still I kept an even countenance.

As calmly as possible, I answered him, "Sal, the Captain always does things for a reason. Watch the ship, and we'll all discover his intentions."

The Sweet Cutlass hoisted the Jolly Roger, maneuvered to broadside one of the merchants and made to board. The pirate crew swung aboard and quickly took the ship as a prize. From the shore where we waited, we saw the pelf transported to the Sweet Cutlass, and then we saw the merchant ship begin to list. She had been scuttled. The Sweet Cutlass then sailed to get broadside to the other anchored merchantman, whose fate became the same as its twin. It was a very smooth operation all around, and I whistled when the merchantmen were both beneath the water.

Sal's shoulders sagged in dejection because the Captain had been cleverer by far than he had estimated. I saw that his potential moment of glory had come and gone. Sal kicked at the earth and scowled. He was beaten and he knew it.

"There goes your plan to take the two merchantmen, Sal. The Captain divined the same plan as you did. I only hope he knows the dreadnought is on the way."

I noticed that the Sweet Cutlass had now struck the skull and crossbones and this time raised the colors of France. The whaleboat was in the water now, approaching the landing in a straight course, but it contained seven men, far too many to take on an additional six. It could take on one more man, barely.

"So Sal, it looks like the Captain has countermanded his own decision about shipping you and yours aboard." This news did not make Sal happy. He and his mates got a sour look as if a grand plan had gone awry. As it neared shore, I realized that the Captain was not in the whaleboat. Rafe jumped on the landing and walked right over for a quiet chat with me.

"The Captain says that Sal is part of a plot to board and sink the Sweet Cutlass. He sent the mates with me to take care of Sal and his men properly. So while you gather whatever rum is left, we'll be executing the Captain's orders."

All that was left of the rum was the keg that Sal had commandeered. I took possession of the keg and stowed it in the whaleboat while Rafe had Sal and his mates strip naked in the street. He tied the men together and arranged them sitting in a star pattern with their backs inside and their legs pointing outwards. Rafe and the mates poured honey over the men until they were covered in the gooey mess, attracting all manner of flies, bees and ants. The captives were becoming extremely uncomfortable, squirming in their discomfort. Then Rafe applied the finishing touch, signs with strings to hang around the five men's necks. Each read, "Pirate."

Admiring his work, Rafe signaled that it was time for us to make our way back to the Sweet Cutlass. As we did that, Sal realized too late that he had no further chance. He shook his head and tried his best to look forlorn. When he saw this had no effect on us, he dropped his façade of joviality and glared. He made the mistake of saying, "Tell the Captain I'll watch him hang for what we just witnessed off this shore."

That was too much for me. Without thinking for a moment about drawing attention by the executions, I aimed my pistol and shot Sal dead between the eyes. I then snatched Rafe's pistol and shot another victim dead between the eyes. The mates understood the game, so they shot the three others. "Now," I said, "we'll see who tells about our pirate work. Rafe, a dreadnought is heading for this port right now. We may have time to escape, but I have doubts. Do you have a signal to alert the Sweet Cutlass in an emergency?"

"Indeed I do, Abe; a great red flag and a pole to mount it on. The Captain said he would be looking for it through his spyglass—just in case."

"So give the signal now. And we'll get in the whaleboat and row for open water and our planned emergency rendezvous."

Rafe's red flag waved, and the Sweet Cutlass fired a cannon to signal its understanding. The ship headed slowly out of the anchorage and turned south while the whaleboat steered a course to intercept. On the horizon to the north was the rigging of the dreadnought, which would make the anchorage just as Sal said it would—unless it gave chase to the Sweet Cutlass instead. I figured that the dreadnought would not give chase for two reasons; it might not be able to identify the south-bound ship as the Sweet Cutlass, and its officers might be looking forward to a night of R&R on the town far more than they looked forward to dying while trying to waylay our pirate ship.

I got a wild idea, and ordered the whaleboat to do wide circles in the water waiting for the dreadnought to set anchor. I briefed the hearties and saw their looks of apprehension turn to wild surmise.

The dreadnought chose to anchor, and its whaleboat set out almost immediately for shore. Our whaleboat closed on the dreadnought silently after dark. We boarded the dreadnought without the ship's sounding an alarm, and we cut the throats of the unwary watch team. We fanned out to do our dirty piratical work, turning one cannon towards the bridge, another at a down angle to hit well below the waterline and a third to hit near the magazine. First we set fires everywhere, and then we ignited the cannon. Those below decks raced topside when the cannons fired, and we laid the marines low with our pistols until we had run out of ammunition. Without missing a beat, we drew our swords and cut them down. The ship was aflame and began to list from taking on water.

I called for my hearties to make their way fighting to the fantail where our whaleboat lay. We had all climbed aboard when the dreadnought's magazine exploded, tearing the ship in two and sending it straight to the bottom.

By firelight I could see that the water was full of debris, bodies, and men swimming for their lives. Any man unfortunate enough to near our whaleboat we skewered with our swords. I surveyed our handiwork and saw that it was good. Not good was the imminent return of the dreadnought's own whaleboat.

Taking a dagger between my teeth, I slipped into the water. As one whaleboat closed on the other, I saw the flashes and heard the reports of rifle and pistol fire that cut down half of my hearties on our whaleboat. Making my way to the rear of the dreadnought's whaleboat, I could barely make out the officer in charge. My dagger flew through the man's neck, and he fell into the water. I pulled my dagger out of the man's neck and closed his whaleboat again, where I threw the dagger at the heart of the man who was giving the orders. I dove under the boat as the remaining three soldiers fired blindly at the water on the opposite side, where I no longer floated. Out of nowhere my whaleboat rammed the dreadnought's whaleboat, and Rafe and two others jumped from one boat to the other to kill the three remaining men.

When all was quiet, I began singing my favorite pirate's song, and all I heard was Rafe laughing and finally saying, "So you survived, you bastard! For a while I thought I was going to be First Mate. No such luck. Now climb aboard and let's blow this anchorage and make that rendezvous with the Captain. He'll be glad that this dreadnought won't be pursuing us tomorrow or any other day." I was amused by Rafe's jibes. I knew he was teasing me, but he was also playing with fire by testing my patience. My respect depended on my rising above his insinuations.

We were four souls aboard the whaleboat as we approached the Sweet Cutlass, and the pirate ship watch was better than the dreadnought's had been. We had a parole, which I had taken pains to master. When the watchmen said, "Bottle." We answered, "Rum." Once we were aboard, our celebrations commenced immediately as we drank from the keg provided by our old pirate shipmate Sal Coinder, may his soul rest forever in Davy Jones' Locker.

Chapter Two
Pirates of Hatteras

*T*he Sweet Cutlass plied the waters off Hatteras, taking treasure and sending merchantmen to Davy Jones' Locker in all seasons, and I was First Mate under the most successful, ruthless and daring pirate of all time. We had just relieved two French merchantmen of their gold and silver, their silk and lace, and their gunpowder and rum, not to mention their ensigns, so we decided to head inland to put our treasure into our secret treasury while our mates prepared for the next merchant that might pass our way. It was good that the Captain made that decision; as we slipped inland, we spied on the horizon a military ship whose mission might be to hunt us down and hang us all.

So we anchored in the sound just west of the spit that separated the bounding main to the east and the brackish, stagnant water of the sound to the west. There swarms of black flies and mosquitoes usually plagued us when the wind was down, but that day we had gusty wind and variable squalls of rain that cut the heat and drove the insects for cover.

The Captain, Rafe, a young recruit named Jamey and I stowed the chest with our treasure and two spades and boarded the whaleboat. We shoved off from the ship and rowed through the reedy area until the ship was out of sight, and then we took our bearings and steered an intentionally crooked course to our goal—a hummock with a willow tree on the far side of the sound where we pulled ashore.

The Captain said, "I don't need a treasure map to discover what I'm looking for." He stood back to the willow with his foot on a gnarled main root of that old tree, and he counted off seven paces due north, then three paces to the west.

"Rafe and Jamey, dig in this place a five-foot-deep hole large enough for a small man's body and a casket."

While the two hearties swung their elbows in the driving rain and the black earth swelled into a growing pile, the Captain drew out a bottle of rum and took a swig, then handed the bottle to me. We exchanged the bottle until the rum was gone, and by then the rain had stopped for a while and the pit had been excavated.

The Captain then drew out a second bottle of rum, and when he had taken a long pull, he offered the bottle to Rafe, who did the same and handed it to Jamey. While the young man drank, the Captain drew his pistol and expertly shot Jamey through the heart. Jamey had no idea this was going to happen. Of course, the rest of the crew knew this would be the result of his accompanying us. I had no remorse about betraying Jamey at the time. Indeed, I no longer think much of it. The pirate's life is hard. The Captain gestured for Rafe and me to place the chest in the hole and to fold Jamey's body around the chest as we always did.

As Rafe and I filled in the hole with the same dirt that had been taken from it, the Captain drank the remainder of the rum while he sang the pirate's song ending in, "Yo ho ho and a bottle of rum." At his urging we joined the Captain in singing the refrain.

When our shoveling work was done, we cut rushes and other greenery and covered the grave so that when we had finished, you could not tell a grave had been placed there. We made sure that we picked up our empty rum bottles and washed our spades in the water around the whaleboat. As we climbed aboard and shoved off, another squall hit us.

In torrential rain we retraced our maze-like path back through the reeds to the Sweet Cutlass, where we discovered that a mutiny was afoot. As we approached, I saw that all the men seemed to be clustered around one side of the ship. Roscoe and some of the others were yelling and cat-calling indistinctly.

Roscoe the Third Mate called out to us through the pouring rain, "I've now taken charge of the ship. All the hearties are with me in my mutiny."

The Captain made a sign to Rafe and me, so we set daggers in our teeth and slipped out of the whaleboat into the water on either side, leaving the Captain to row the rest of the way alone to the ship.

While the Captain exchanged words with the Third Mate, Rafe and I swam separately to the focsle and fantail where we climbed aboard by ropes that hung over the sides. As we figured, Roscoe and the crew were all huddled on the port side watching and listening to the dialog between the Captain in the whaleboat and Roscoe the Third Mate by the gangway ladder strung over the side amidships.

The Captain was pretending to be drunk, and he continued to sing pirate songs until he was within five yards of Roscoe, who was suddenly confused by seeing that the Captain was alone. His plan counted on the Captain, me the First Mate and the Second Mate to be killed together.

"Aye, Third Mate, you're wondering where the First Mate, the Second Mate and young Jamey have gone. Well, treasure requires souls of dead men to guard it, and they volunteered to provide the souls. If you find them—which I sincerely doubt you will, you'll find them all with their arms around the treasure back where I came from. And I confess I drank all the rum we took along to ease our labors, so I'll thank you for fetching me a fresh bottle now to slake my thirst while we discuss this mutiny of yours."

Roscoe was used to obeying orders, so he fetched a bottle and threw it down gently. The Captain caught it in his hand, pulled the cork plug with his teeth and spat the cork out. With a single motion he raised the bottle to his lips and drew and fired his pistol. Roscoe fell dead into the water between the ship and the whaleboat.

The Captain wiped his mouth with his sleeve, "Who's now in charge of this mutiny?"

Meanwhile, Rafe and I had snuck up behind the crew so that when a burly lout named Daniel stepped forward to take Roscoe's place and a strongman named Whiskers stepped forward and took issue with Daniel's attempt to assume leadership, we grabbed those men from behind. Without pausing, we neatly slit their throats and pushed their gurgling bodies into the waters of the sound.

"I cannot hear who is to be your leader!" the Captain said, holding one hand to his good ear, the one with the gold earring.

I answered for all, "Captain, come aboard, for you're the only rightful leader of this pirate crew. If anyone objects, he'll have to answer to Rafe and me. Hearties, do I hear any objections? No? So everyone forget about this mutiny and get back to preparing this pirate ship for battle. With all these newly dead souls, your share of treasure has become fit for a king, but I dare say the share of the dead goes to the Captain to distribute or not as he sees fit."

"Well spoken, Abe," the Captain said. "Mates and all hearties, prepare to sail and stand by to weigh anchor in ten minutes."

The mates flew to their tasks with alacrity while the Captain climbed aboard to share his rum with Rafe and me. He mounted to the bridge in a pensive mood that boded no good and watched his men with dour regard.

I thought he was looking for any sign of dissent or disgruntlement, but I was wrong. He was instead assessing who naturally filled the role of the now-deceased Roscoe, and he called one sturdy man named Samuel before the mast. Sam stood tall but humbly before his Captain, uncertain why he had been summoned. The Captain told Sam he had two choices. Either he could accept the office of Third Mate with the Third Mate's share, or he could dive into the water and swim with the other bodies to the nearest shore of Hell and remain there marooned forever.

Sam made the wise choice and became our Third Mate. To celebrate, the Captain asked Sam to take a swig of rum. Then the Captain announced his decision to the crew and asked for a cheer and a song for the new Third Mate.

When the cheering, singing and general revelry were over, the Captain gave the orders to hoist the whaleboat on its davits, unfurl the Jolly Roger and get the ship underway. The Captain gave me the first watch. We then processed cheerily through the inlet to the sea, with a new following wind that seemed providential on a day that had claimed more than its share of pirate lives.

As our luck would have it, as we reached the bounding main the lookout immediately shouted, "Ship Ahoy!"

The Captain answered, "Where away?"

The lookout called out, "Two points abaft the port bow."

There through our spyglasses the Captain and I sighted another French merchantman on the horizon, and when the Captain gave the order, we raced to intercept her, with constant bearing and decreasing range, all sails set and the crew ready to plunder as much for riches as for atonement for a mutiny that had run foul.

We overtook the French merchant after another squall drenched the ocean with rain and left our ship washed clean like a spring lamb. Sunlight streaked through the clouds as we came about to meet the merchant broadside. The ship had wisely raised the white flag of surrender. We eased right alongside and the crew flew with swords and knives drawn to the main deck of the merchant. There we met with no resistance.

A quick search of the prize ship yielded a hoard of treasure including gold and silver bars and coin. Below decks on the merchant ship the crew found four dozen tuns of rum and another four of wine, all of which were raised and high-lined to the Sweet Cutlass for stowage below in our hold. When the treasure and everything else worth taking had been removed from the French ship, the Captain made a magnanimous, eloquent and mercifully brief speech about mercy, fortune and Our Maker.

Then he laughed maliciously and called all pirates back to the Sweet Cutlass. When the hearties had all returned, the Captain, with a flourish of his tricorn, let the merchantman proceed wherever it pleased and ordered the Sweet Cutlass back to its duty patrolling the waters off Hatteras.

We took no more plunder that day, which continued to alternate between squalls and sunshine, until at evening the sea became becalmed as if it were a lake. Now as Rafe relieved me of the watch, the moonshine from a gibbous moon streamed its silver reflection over the unfathomable depths.

The smoking lamp was lit, and as I smoked my pipe I reflected on chance and fate and my growing esteem for the Captain who had shown no fear in the face of mutiny and no squeamishness about the sacred pirate duty to offer a sacrifice to his treasure.

For the next four weeks, the Sweet Cutlass took its pleasure from the booty taken from ten merchantmen. We lost only one pirate soul during that interval, and the example lives with me as an omen today.

We had drawn alongside a German merchantman that had raised the white flag of surrender. Instead of docilely allowing us to take our pelf and withdraw unhindered, the perfidious Hun Captain cut down the first pirate aboard his ship with his cutlass.

The Captain, seeing what had happened in violation of every protocol and law of the sea, drew his pistol and shot the German Captain dead through the forehead. He then ordered all the crew of the prize ship to be assembled on the focsle of their vessel. At the Captain's order, I took charge of the proceedings that followed.

I swung by line to the main deck of the German ship and said that the crew should strip themselves naked. Meanwhile, I ordered all stores of meat and fish to be brought topside and a plank to be erected to the windward side of the ship. As the meat and fish arrived topside, I had the pirate hearties chum with it off the leeward side until the blue waters boiled with ravenous sharks that tore into the chum and each other so that the water ran with blood, drawing even more sharks and other fish to the feast.

When the entire hoard of chum had been off-boarded, I ordered that the German crew be brought one naked man at a time to walk the plank. As the pink flesh hit the water body by body, the sharks flew into ecstasy and a feeding frenzy. The sea soup of limbs and waving heads and hands, the cries of agony and pain, and the cries of gulls and other sea birds created a sonorous and visual symphony, a lesson for all who watched.

When the last German crew member had walked the plank to meet his Maker, I asked, "Do any of you pirate crew want to join the Germans in the deep?" I knew more than one whom I would have liked to say, "Aye, me!"

No one volunteered.

I ordered the pirates to go below decks to the German hold and use whatever means they could find to breach the vessel so that it could join the numberless other vessels down in the locker at the bottom of the sea. With a common yell, the pirates did just that, and they came back to the main decks saying that the German ship was sinking fast. I ordered all pirates to return to the Sweet Cutlass, where we mended our kit and prepared for our next conquest while the German vessel sank below the waves, scattering flotsam all around our windward side.

That evening the Captain called a meeting of the Mates before the mast. There he said, "We have been fortunate during this season, but luck can run its course. We'll take on stores, rest and prepare for further adventures." He announced that the ship would break off from patrol off Hatteras and set sail at once for San Juan, where we would port in and get a little time ashore.

While the Third Mate took the watch, the Captain took Rafe and me aside and said, "Look alive in the meantime, hearties, and watch both the Third Mate and the crew."

"Aye, Captain, but will watching be enough?" Rafe asked.

"The lesson of watching that German crew walk the plank should suffice to keep them in line, but only time will tell. Now let's fetch some rum and carouse till midnight. It truly is a beautiful night."

The Captain was, as always, right; I noticed how the phosphors glistened, all silver and purple in our wake.

Chapter Three
Pirates of the Bermudas

*T*he Sweet Cutlass plied the waters off the Bermudas, taking treasure and enjoying the sunshine and the sea. We rose and fell in swells that soared forty feet from trough to top with waves as clear as glass windows. In the trough you could see the wisps of green seaweed against the cerulean, flitting schools of colorful fish and, sometimes, a great white shark swimming with a man's arm or leg in its mouth, a grim reminder of a recent raid. Along the ship's weather decks flying fish landed and, if they were lucky, skittered down one of the scuppers and slid back into the main. A school of porpoises swam by as if driven by some invisible sea god, and high above the white clouds were urged on by winds that sang in our rigging and swelled our sails.

Today we flew the colors of Spain pretending to be a merchantman, and we lay in wait for one specific ship that we knew to be unusually full of rich pelf; the pirate vessel Amazonia captained by Captain Mordalia, the most feared female pirate in the world. Captain Morgan, our skipper, was intrigued with Mordalia's legend because her mates were said to be bloodthirsty women like herself. With a leer the Captain told me that we would board the Amazonia, seize everything of value, have our will with the women and then send the Amazonia and the Amazons down to Davy Jones's locker.

We sighted the Amazonia on the horizon at constant bearing, decreasing range. While she closed on us, the Captain ordered everyone to look lively and hide the weapons and grappling hooks. The closing ship was flying the Jolly Roger, sure enough, and it fired a warning shot across our bow.

The Captain ordered us to luff sail, come about and prepare for boarding. As we came about, the Captain ordered us to haul down the Spanish colors and raise the Jolly Roger. Now it was apparent to the Amazonia that the game was pirate-to-pirate and winner-take-all.

The Amazonia did not falter in its progress and continued to close as we came dead in the water and waited. With his spyglass the Captain assessed the action aboard the Amazonia, and he exclaimed when that ship luffed sail and came about in parallel with the Sweet Cutlass around five hundred yards abeam.

Seeing that the Amazonia was about to launch a whaleboat with its skipper aboard, he ordered us to prepare his own whaleboat and swing it out on its davits. He then gave me his spyglass and the watch, and he leapt into his boat as it was lowered into the undulating sea. While the two pirate ships rose up and down in the ocean, the two whaleboats closed and came right alongside each other between the ships, and the coxswains rose to tether the two boats together.

There between our ships the pirate Captains held a gam, the ancient tradition of Captains the world over. Captain Morgan gallantly saluted Captain Mordalia, who in mockery of tradition, curtsied and gestured for him to come aboard her boat to share a keg of rum she had brought to lubricate their chat.

Our Captain went aboard and the two began to drink and talk and laugh and nudge each other and laugh some more.

I was anxious about the Captain's security, and I saw through the spyglass that the First Mate aboard the Amazonia was similarly worried for her Captain. The Captains regaled each other and toasted and drank until their keg of rum was empty. Then the Captains embraced heartily and clapped each other on the arm. They laughed and gestured while Captain Morgan climbed back aboard his boat.

The whaleboats disjoined and were rowed back to the ships they came from. Captain Morgan sprang from his whaleboat and shouted for everyone to prepare to board the Amazonia immediately. I saw that the Amazonia was now making all preparations to fight and board as well. As always, a friendly pirate meeting was turning into a contest with Davy Jones' Locker as the final destination.

So after the pleasantries and the rum, we were hell bent on mutual destruction. The two ships were now coming to full sail and heading straight at each other. As if synchronized to the minute, both ships came about at the same time. The crews from both ships swung to the other with knives clenched in teeth, cutlasses swinging and grappling hooks flying from one deck to the other. A few pistol shots were fired, and the pitched battle seethed. The two ships became tethered together, riding in tandem the great waves that swept them up and down in the forty-foot swells. Men and women screamed bloody murder, and pirates swung aboard while pistols fired and swords slashed in all directions.

Each Captain, having taken position by the helm, watched and shouted orders above the din. Then I went below to execute our secret strategy for close ship-to-ship combat. I lighted the fuse of the cannon we rigged there for scuttling a vessel that had come right alongside. The cannon's loud report was answered by creaking and groaning aboard the Amazonia as she began to take on water.

Now Captain Mordalia ordered her entire crew over the side to board the Sweet Cutlass, hazarding all lives on taking our ship. Desperation drove the fight now as the Amazons flew aboard on ropes from above and along the railings with our crew working hard to repel them. Captain Morgan ordered all our mates who were aboard the Amazonia to return at once or be left to his fate on the sinking ship. He ordered me to cut all lines that bound the two ships, and I did so, battling the women pirates as I progressed.

I noticed that the two Captains were locked in mortal combat beside the helm, and they were left to fend for themselves since everyone else had his own match to fight. I sliced a woman in half as she was about to slay our second mate, and I cut off the arm of another who would have ended the life of the Captain's cabin boy.

Captain Morgan pressed Captain Mordalia to the rail and caused her to fall backwards overboard, still holding her knife and sword. My Captain did not hesitate but fixed his knife in his teeth and dived into the ocean after her. The two grappled in the water and then went down. Because the water was so clear, every time we sank into the trough, we could see the two Captains fighting each other underwater with their legs kicking, their knives thrusting and their hands trying to get a good purchase on the other's hair. I did not know how either combatant could hold breath as long as they did, and I thought one must surely drown before the fight ended. Then as we went down, I saw that each Captain had the other by their long hair and had pulled their heads back and readied their knives for the final slice. We rose again before we saw the end of the fight, but when we fell into the next trough, I saw Captain Morgan thrusting his arms to get to the surface while a second body rose of its own accord. The Captain had something in his hand. When he broke the surface, he gasped and sputtered. Then he raised his right hand above the water. In his fist was a tangle of wet hair attached to the decapitated head of Captain Mordalia.

I grabbed a grappling hook and threw it beyond Captain Morgan's position, and he grasped the line so that I could pull him in. He stood in the grappling hook so we could haul him on deck to watch the final rout of the adversary. He still held Captain Mordalia's head by the hair and brandished it as if he were Perseus holding Medusa's snaky locks on high. A cheer went up from my hearties, and the Amazons despaired because their leader had died so ignobly.

At this time the Amazonia, now flooded to the limit, sank below the water and rapidly descended to the bottom. Another cheer went up led by our Second Mate, who immediately slew three women pirates with well-placed thrusts of his sword. The slicing and hacking continued until, one by one, the Amazons joined their leader in the cerulean water, which now was so full of blood that sharks had come to feast. The sharks came not in singles but in swarms and multitudes. They fed in frenzy, ripping flesh apart and taking limbs so as to drag whole corpses away. The sharks were so excited that they began to eat each other.

"See, Rafe," I called out with a chuckle, "how the cannibal feast of sharks is emblematic of us pirates slaying other pirates."

"Aye, Abe, all that's missing is the rum." He laughed heartily as he watched the infernal feast.

In the ocean swells I saw flotsam from the sunken Amazonia, women's hair extending from some bodies, and body parts being fought over by ravenous predators. I soberly reflected that our dead and wounded as well as the Amazons were part of the feast.

The last surviving Amazon fought so fiercely and well that Captain Morgan stopped the fight to give the woman the chance to surrender and live. I thought the Captain was the model of chivalry. He had assumed a regal pose from some heroic painting, but his act was all in vain.

She looked at him defiantly, threw her knife into the air, caught the blade descending and expertly hurled the weapon at Captain Morgan. He saw her intent and raised the head of Captain Mordalia, which received the poniard in its swollen eye where it stuck like an insult. The Captain nodded to the Second Mate, who swept his sword through the woman's neck.

I grabbed the head by the hair as the woman's bleeding body hit the deck. The fight was truly over, and Captain Morgan handed Captain Mordalia's head to me to dispose of. So while he gave orders to muster the survivors and clean ship, I held two heavy heads wondering how to proceed. I found two net bags into which I placed the women pirates' heads and tied the bags together with line. Then I jammed a grappling hook into the mainmast and over the hooks put the line between the bags. The Captain could now see the two heads whenever he stood by the helm as a reminder of their victory over the Amazonia.

At sunset we still saw shark fins cutting the waters all around the ship, and other fish that were scared by the behemoths leapt out of the water and scattered all over our decks. The Captain liked for the ship to sail into the sunset, and that we did until the light failed completely. At that time he ordered the helmsman to steer due south for Bermuda where, he promised, the crew would be treated to a rest with plenty of rum.

That evening the Captain held a meeting of the three mates, and we reviewed the day's events. Captain Morgan told us that Captain Mordalia had been valiant, but she was hairy all over and stank. He opined that her final swim might have been her only bath in the last six months. He told us that they had discussed much during their gam. She had told him about an approaching convoy of French merchantmen and offered a deal for the two pirate ships to work together. He had laughed at the offer and asked the female pirate whether the Amazonia could hold more gold and silver than it already carried. In answering him, she smiled and said that she had plenty of room since she had stopped on Bermuda and buried her pelf where no one could possibly find it. She did not know at the time that her confession sealed the fate of her, her crew and her ship.

Taking a long draught of rum, Captain Morgan got a glint in his eye and said he never worked together with anyone in piracy and never would do so. He claimed it was a matter of honor. So he told Captain Mordalia that he and his men would fight her and her Amazons to the very end, giving no quarter. With a sneer he promised he would cut off her head and hold it high by the hair. She had laughed as if he must be joking, and she endeared herself to him always when she told him she would race him back to his ship and then come alongside to board, scuttle and sink the Sweet Cutlass. Of course, the Captain had no regret about killing her.

At first light the next morning, we sighted the Bermudian reefs and we sailed to anchor in the shelter of a little bay where the whaleboat took the crew in shifts to the pure white sands of shore. The Captain asked me to leave the Second Mate in charge of the ship, bring the cabin boy and three spades and come with him on a treasure hunt. So we went around the island in the whaleboat until we reached an inlet that the Captain seemed to know. We rowed up the inlet until we saw an odd growth of palm trees as if three trees had grown from the same root stock, one straight up and the two others out to the right and left. The palms naturally formed Poseidon's trident. We beached the whaleboat and climbed out with our spades, and I knew why the Captain had chosen this spot.

The Captain surveyed the ground around the palms, and he saw a large, round stone directly east of the configuration. He paced the distance from the trident to the stone and took the same number of paces from the trident to the west, away from the stone and on the other side of the trident where there was no marker.

Laughing, he ordered, "Now Abe and cabin boy, dig here."

He pulled out a bottle of rum and drank while he supervised us. We dug until blisters formed on our hands, and the Captain picked up the third spade and joined us in digging. We excavated an area five feet deep, and water was beginning to seep into our hole when I struck something solid that turned out to be the skull of a man that still sported long hair and a beard.

I held up the skull and smiled. The Captain laughed.

Directly below that skull we found a chest. The Captain nodded sagely and told us that we should raise the top of the chest.

When we finished, under the water we saw the glitter of gold and the black of oxidized silver. The Captain ordered the cabin boy to pick up three dozen gold coins, and then he asked us to replace the lid of the chest, restore the skull where we had found it and fill in the hole we had made in the sand.

He directed us to remove any trace of our having dug in this place. This was hard work even though the Captain helped us do it. We completed our work and shoved off in the whaleboat at sunset. We made our way back around the island to find the others had tired of their liberty and returned to the ship. Some of the crew were gathered on the focsle telling stories of their prowess during the fight. Others were gathered around a pirate playing a mournful song on a homemade flute. Two pirates who I knew were recluses were smoking shanks of hemp on the fantail and meditating on the vagaries of fortune.

A kind of hospital had been fashioned below decks, where I found the three men who had been savagely cut during the fight. One had lost his arm beneath the shoulder. Another had lost his leg beneath the knee. The third had lost an eye and part of his upper face. I took out my knife and stabbed the two who had lost their limbs because they were no longer useful. I had no regrets. Good men, they understood the pirate code I executed. What good is life when a man is not hearty?

The man with one eye I spared, because if he lived he could still manage the hard pirate's work ahead. I ordered two of the crew to haul the fresh corpses topside where they were wrapped in canvas, which was sewn shut. When I had told the Captain that the crew was ready now, he made the rounds of all the crew, and into each survivor's hand he placed one golden coin from the hoard that we had visited. I received a coin that night along with all the others, and I kept it with me on a chain around my neck. That night I had to remain aboard the ship to stand my watch, and as I watched the stars appear in all their majesty, I tried to memorize our current position by a celestial fix so I could find it again on another excursion. The Captain, the cabin boy and I were the only shipmates who knew where the gold coins had been unearthed. Who knew what fate would bring?

The next day we set sail at first light with a breeze that seemed to favor our transiting the Bermudas. When the Captain reached a certain spot just north of the main island, he trained his spyglass on the port and directed the ship to anchor out on his mark. When he was sure the anchor was well set, he left me in charge of the ship while he and the Second Mate took the whaleboat to the wharf. They were gone for an hour and returned so the Second Mate could relieve me, and I took his place alongside the Captain for his second run to the shore.

Captain Morgan and I walked through the main street to a run-down, storm-damaged hut on the edge of the Bermudian settlement. Dogs lay in the street outside the hut, and two boys played in a side yard to the house across the street. The Captain asked me to keep watch outside while he entered the hut. He asked me to keep custody of his bottle of rum, and he suggested that I could take a swig or two to slake my thirst in the hot sun. The Captain remained inside the hut for over two hours, and when he emerged again, he had a faraway look in his eye.

I figured he would let me know what I needed to know in due course, so I asked no questions and accompanied him back to the whaleboat and then to the Sweet Cutlass, still at anchor. When we were aboard, Captain Morgan called a meeting of the mates and explained that we were now going to take our pick of French merchantmen that were expected to anchor here soon. He ordered us to raise again the Spanish colors and to warn every crew member to look sharp and be ready for action on a moment's notice.

The Captain took me aside and confided that the now-dead Captain Mordalia's intelligence had been spot-on about the advent of the French ships. The woman he had visited in the hut had confirmed it. She was the crone called the Sea Hag of the Bermudas, and she was never known to lie. The Captain told me that the Sea Hag still smelled as bad as she ever did, and she swore and cursed when she discovered that her daughter and her protégé Captain Mordalia had been killed. Mordalia was her daughter by a French nobleman who had visited Bermuda over thirty years ago. He said it was all he could do to prevent her from trying to wreak vengeance. To calm the woman, the Captain had to give her twenty gold coins, but she continued to curse him, his crew and his ship. Captain Morgan was not fearful of many things in this world, but the curses of the Sea Hag made him melancholic in the extreme.

"Captain, why didn't you kill the woman summarily?"

He scowled and answered, "Her death would not remove her curse once it was uttered. I still need a source of intelligence in the Bermudas, and I don't know anyone else capable of doing the job. I didn't know Captain Mordalia was the crone's daughter, but what's done is done. Now we have to weather any ill effects that will come of her curse. Rum can help." He said this with a sardonic chuckle and a shake of his head. With that thought, he retired to his cabin with two bottles of rum. Before he slept, he ordered me to inform him of the arrival of the French merchant ships.

The French arrived just before sunset, and they anchored all around us. The Captains of those ships all went ashore in their whaleboats with a third of their crews, and those who remained aboard the ships were totally unsuspicious of the lone Spanish ship that also occupied the anchorage. I informed the Captain, who was clearly drunk but still lucid. He told me to take our whaleboat ashore and destroy all the whaleboats of the French merchant ships and return. I took five of our crew with me, and we made short work of the whaleboats without raising any ruckus or alarming those who had gone ashore. When we returned to the Sweet Cutlass, the Captain seemed to have recovered completely from his drunkenness. He gave orders that made complete sense and answered every question I would have asked beforehand.

The Captain's plan was to take out the watch teams of each of the French merchants, one by one. I was to handpick the men who would go aboard each ship to do the job and drop each off so that no one raised the alarm on any ship. I took my bow and arrows as a silent means of eliminating each watch officer. Once all the watch teams had been eliminated, I was to find a way to set the largest ship on fire and sink it if I could. I was then to take my team to each of the other ships, kill the crew and seize anything of value. The Captain said that as I completed the plunder of each ship, I should leave one man to sabotage and sink it.

The Captain's plan went like clockwork. First we eliminated the watch at each of the ships in turn. No alarms were raised, so we were ready for the second phase of the operation. We then took the largest ship by surprise, overcame the few crew members who emerged from below decks, and barricaded the rest of the crew in their quarters. Then we went to the hold and planted a keg of gunpowder with a lighted fuse. After we shoved off in our whaleboat, the gunpowder exploded, blowing a hole in the vessel's bottom and setting the ship afire. The ship burned for a while and sank like a stone. When all but the top of the ship's mast was above water, we had arrived at the next ship, where we ignored the crew who had gathered to watch the burning ship. We snuck below decks to look for plunder in the ship's stores. We found rum aplenty, gold and silver, and textiles. The men took what they could carry and stole over the side while I set the charge that would sink the vessel like the first we had sunk. I had to kill two of the crew as I made my escape, but no one sounded the alarm as we pulled away in our whaleboat.

We proceeded to the next ship as the charge went off, and we witnessed another bonfire and saw another ship sink to become the stub of a mast. This time some of the crew were swimming and holding on to pieces of the wreckage of their ship. I looked towards the port area, and I saw that a crowd had gathered but no one was able to use any of the boats we had scuttled. I also looked towards the Sweet Cutlass, where I spied the Captain's personal distress signal. Barely in the darkness I saw that the sails were set and the ship was moving. I nudged the oarsman to aim for the Sweet Cutlass because our escapade had been curtailed.

"Colin, take charge of this whaleboat. Row directly to the Sweet Cutlass and tell the Captain I'll catch up with the ship later."

On the way past one of the two remaining French merchants, I put a knife between my teeth and slipped out of the whaleboat and into the water.

I swam to the rope ladder that hung down to just above the waterline and climbed aboard. I encountered no opposition because the entire crew was lining the rail, fixated on the second sinking vessel. For the third time that night, I planted a charge in the hold of a merchantman and lit the fuse. I made it back topside, put my knife back in my mouth and dove into the water as the charge went off. I did not look back but swam to the last French merchant, where again I climbed the rope ladder to the deck level.

An alert sentry moved right up to me to ask in French, "Why are you coming aboard?"

I replied, "Officer, I was on the merchantman you saw sinking. Isn't that reason enough?"

This bought me enough time to bury my knife in the man's heart. I moved the dead body to the side and let it slip overboard. I then did what I had done on the last ship, lit the fuse and dove over the side to make for the Sweet Cutlass. When the gunpowder exploded and the ship went up in flames, I saw that the whaleboat was coming right towards me. The Captain himself grabbed my hand and hauled me aboard, clasping my arm after I was seated. The whaleboat returned to our ship, which was now underway. We fastened the davit hooks alongside and sat while the hearties raised us to the deck level. The Captain and I went to the bridge, and I, though soaking wet, relieved the Second Mate of the watch.

We cleared the anchorage as the fourth French ship disappeared below the water. By sunrise, we were well out to sea proceeding north. The Second Mate now relieved me of the watch, and I went to see the Captain in his cabin. There he informed me that he wished he could have allowed me to continue on our plan the night before. The Sea Hag had warned him that she envisioned the Sweet Cutlass sinking only two French ships. Beyond that was not in her purview. Seeing the crowds on the Bermudian shore, Captain Morgan decided that he would not press his luck. So now the Sweet Cutlass was pounding the main again. The gold and silver we had liberated from the one French merchant was honorable spoil for a night's raiding party. The Captain did not know what he was going to do with the fine materials, among which were silk and damask, but he would decide that later.

The Captain asked me, "Who deserves a special reward for the piracy we've committed?"

I told him, "I'm not ashamed to say I didn't know what I was going to do after blowing up the last ship. As I swam I calculated the odds of my swimming to catch our ship, so I was surprised and overjoyed to see our whaleboat coming right at me from out of nowhere. Thank you, Captain, for being there to pick me up."

He sneered at my having been squeamish, and then he laughed out loud. He passed me his bottle of rum, and I drank. He mumbled a few words about my having taken out two more French ships than the Sea Hag had counted.

I said, "We're not much richer for that exploit."

The Captain rejoined, "Even a merchant can be a formidable opponent. Now because of what you've done, we'll not have pursuers while we plan our next piracy. The Sea Hag gave me intelligence about our next target. On our present heading, we'll see a sail dead ahead before sundown today."

Chapter Four
Pirates of Madagascar

*W*e had been taking ships and plenty of pelf off the Canaries until Captain Morgan decided we might be getting too much of a good thing. One bright morning, the Captain ordered the Sweet Cutlass to sail south and east for the Ear of Africa and then to take the slow route south along the west coast of Africa to the Cape of Good Hope. Afterward we would pass through the cold winds and mean rip tides of the crossover at the tip of the cape, to sail up the east coast to Madagascar.

Not all the crew was happy with this plan, and the Third Mate and two others asked to be put ashore with their share of our current booty. The Captain, always the perfect democrat, called all crew topside to adjudicate the matter. So there the ship lay with its sails furled against a gentle breeze with the Captain and me up by the wheel and the crew gathered down around the mast.

The Captain calmly asked the Third Mate to tell the crew what he and his two companions wished to do and why. The Third Mate was unruffled, and he said he reckoned that the Sweet Cutlass had gathered as much treasure as was possible during the last four months around the Canaries. He said the month-long voyage around the cape would not be commensurately profitable, so he and his hearties figured they would take their share of what had been gathered now and jump ship. He explained that they would ship aboard some other vessel and continue to work here near the Canaries. Maybe, he said, they would ship back aboard the Sweet Cutlass when it returned from Madagascar—if that ever happened.

The Captain seemed to take seriously what his Third Mate said and nodded his head throughout the man's case as if he was impressed with the plan. When the Third Mate had finished and swelled up with pride for having done well articulating his plan, the Captain asked the crew whether any other of them wanted to join the Third Mate and his two hearties. The crew was silent and suspicious because they knew their Captain's calculating moods. The Captain said he reckoned from their silence that that the Third Mate and his two hearties were the only pirates on the ship who were in the deal. His voice boomed out that this was the last call to join the Third Mate or to remain with the Sweet Cutlass on its new voyage to Madagascar. No one answered the Captain's call to join the Third Mate. In fact, the crew shuffled back a few steps to distance themselves from the Third Mate and his two confederates so that those three men stood alone before the mast.

Then the Captain asked me as First Mate what the death of a crew member meant with regard to each man's share. I answered that the dead man's share belonged in equal part to the remaining crew. The Captain nodded and asked what each living man should deduce from that fundamental maxim of pirates everywhere.

I said, "More for the rest of us."

With a dangerous chuckle the Captain rose to his full height and ordered the Second Mate to shove out the plank on the lee side of the vessel, because three men had opted to leave the ship and he intended to give them a good send off.

A commotion stirred among the crew while the plank was shoved out over the side. The crew knew the meaning of that plank, for many of their victims had walked off it at sword point into the sea.

The Third Mate had now turned pale, and his two hearties were fidgeting back and forth. They seemed to be having second thoughts about their rash decision to join the man in his pig-headed undertaking. The Captain cheerily asked the three mutineers who would like to mount the plank first.

While they were deliberating among each other, he ordered the Second Mate to chum the waters on the side of the vessel where the plank extended. He ordered me to draw and cock my pistol and to maintain order during the proceedings, as he was going to withdraw to his quarters for a moment to relieve himself.

The Captain went back towards his cabin while I assumed the Conn and kept watch over the crew. Meanwhile the first fins cut through the clear, calm water where the chum had fallen. Soon the water would be a chaos of sharks seeking blood with their wide mouths open, and the crew became fascinated with the thought of the feast we would soon provide for them.

The Third Mate called me by my name, "Abe, will you intervene with the Captain in our behalf? I beseech you for mercy." He quailed as our victims invariably had done before they had walked the plank. "I deserve my share and my hearties also deserve theirs."

As if he had heard this plea, the Captain emerged from his cabin with three sacks, which he held up so that all the crew could see.

"In these sacks," the Captain said, "are the shares of loot that you departing men earned."

He turned to the crew and said, "Each sack contains gold and silver coins."

He opened one sack and grabbed a fistful of coins and flung it to the deck below so the crew could see the truth of what he said for themselves. No one touched the coins, though there was no mistaking the glittering coins for anything but gold and silver.

The Captain said, "The crew must decide what will happen to the bags of pelf, as man by man the Third Mate and his hearties leave the ship."

The first man to the plank was the Third Mate himself. The Second Mate bound the condemned man's hands and escorted him to the end of the plank, where he looked down into gently undulating ocean water boiling with hungry sharks.

When the man was in position, the Captain raised a sack and asked the crew, "Is it fair to give the Third Mate his share knowing his fate?"

When none of the crew answered his question, the Captain asked me, "Abe, what do you think?"

I said, "Davy Jones has plenty of treasure, but he always likes additional company. Where the Third Mate is going, he'll have more treasure than the Sweet Cutlass had ever conceived of. In that case the pirate rule for sharing the wealth should prevail: 'The more for the rest of us!'"

The crew murmured their agreement with what I said.

The Captain nodded, and he said, "Each man shall make the determination for himself."

He flung all the coins from one bag down on the deck and said, "Each crew member can either keep whatever he picks up or fling it overboard to the Third Mate as he sees fit."

Then he motioned for the Second Mate to edge the Third Mate off the plank.

So at the same time the Third Mate hit the ocean water with its forest of shark fins, the crew hit the ship's decks picking up coins—all but the two hearties of the Third Mate, who stood trembling as the Second Mate approached to bind them for their last walk on earth. Down in the water the Third Mate's body was being torn apart by two gigantic sharks, when a third even larger shark swam between them and took off the man's abdomen with a single bite. The blood and gore in the blue water drove the feeding fish into a feasting frenzy while the Second Mate readied the next man for the plank.

The Captain looked the bound man in the eye and asked him, "Have you trained with the Third Mate so you can one day become Third Mate yourself?"

The man answered, "Aye, Captain!"

The Captain raised a second sack and said, "This is the man's share. Is it now a fair share given what's just happened?" I was about to answer, but the Captain raised his hand to stop me from responding and gestured to the hapless man near the plank to answer his question.

The man looked the Captain steadily in the eye and said, "Captain, with one share re-divided, the amount in the sack, if it be the same as the other that was just distributed, is too small by the amount divided by the number of the crew. So it is not fair."

The Captain looked at the man fiercely and then asked me, "Abe, what do you think of this judgment?"

Without looking at the Captain, I said, "Judgment is a rare commodity among seamen and it's worth much more than gold and silver coins."

The Captain then asked me, "What would you do if you were the ship's Captain under the circumstances?"

I took a few minutes to consider this, and I answered, "If I were you, Captain, I'd offer the choice of the cat-o-nine-tails or the plank, and if he chose the cat, I'd have a tamed Third Mate. If not, I'd have no Third Mate."

The Captain then asked the man near the plank, "Will you choose the cat or the plank?"

The man answered, "Captain, I choose the cat-o-nine-tails but with the proviso that my hearty be given the same choice as me."

The Captain looked down at the seething waters off the lee side of the ship and nodded in acquiescence.

The third man, grateful for his having been granted the chance at life, chose the cat over the plank, and the Captain ordered the plank withdrawn and stowed.

The Captain then ordered the crew to return to their stations on their normal watch routines, all except for the two hearties that were taken by the Second Mate before the mast to sit on the deck and prepare their own cat-o-nine-tails. The Captain returned the two remaining sacks of booty to his cabin while I un-cocked my pistol and shoved it into my belt. I stood the watch as we unfurled the sails and sailed southeast with fair winds and following seas on our cruise to Madagascar.

****

I learned that ocean trade along the West African coast was brisk, and the Sweet Cutlass had its choice of vessels. Most of the trade was conducted in barter, but the trading ships always had some gold and silver aboard. As pirates we had competition that sometimes wanted to prey upon ourselves. So it was as we entered the Bay of Shrimps under the Ear of Africa a pirate ship displaying the Jolly Roger came at us from the shore.

Next to the Sweet Cutlass, our competitor seemed a slovenly scow, but its Captain was no fool and called for a gam with Captain Morgan. The Captain agreed and ordered that his whaleboat be launched for the meeting.

No sooner had the two Captains met between our ships than the pirate vessel fired at the Sweet Cutlass. I was ready for such a ploy, and I ordered all our guns to fire at the main brace of the pirate ship while I saw my Captain draw his knife, leap aboard the whaleboat of the other Captain and slay both the man and his coxswain.

Having destroyed the enemy's main brace, the ship could not maneuver, so I took the Sweet Cutlass alongside and ordered the men to board and take no prisoners. It took almost no time for our crew to dispatch the enemy's crew and throw the bodies into the water. Making the Sweet Cutlass fast to the enemy pirate ship, we took our time plundering it of everything of value, especially the guns, powder, cannon balls and scrap shot. Meanwhile, we winched the Captain's whaleboat back aboard with him and the coxswain inside it.

At the Captain's orders we scuttled the pirate vessel and maneuvered along the shore until we found the village from which the enemy pirates had come. The Captain anchored out and after dark ordered me to take a prize crew to row the whaleboat ashore to reconnoiter.

I steered by the light of a fire near the shore, and we landed the whaleboat amidst a number of boats along the beach. With our weapons, we advanced on the village where the villagers were assembled around the bonfire that we had steered by. I told my hearties to stand back until I called them.

I then proceeded alone to address the villagers, who were startled to see me appear out of nowhere alone with my cocked pistol.

The man in charge of the remnant of the pirate colony laughed at the idea that I would approach him without any apparent reinforcements. When he rose and reached for his own pistol, I shot him through the heart. I called my hearties forward and told the villagers that we had come for treasure and valuables. I said we would do them no harm if they did not resist us, but they decided to take their chances by rushing us with their knives drawn. We slew them all, men and women alike. Then we fashioned torches, lighted them in the bonfire and went from dwelling to dwelling to scout for valuables.

We found the hut that must have belonged to the pirate Captain. It was full of treasure hidden under some carpets in a chest in a hole that had been dug in the center of the earthen floor. We withdrew with that chest, taking care to set all the huts aflame as we departed. We stove in all the boats that lay on the shore in case some pirates who were absent in the jungle might return to pursue us. Then we rowed with our treasure back out to our anchored Sweet Cutlass.

When I presented the chest of treasure to the Captain in his cabin, he smiled and said he thought other pirates lurked all along the coast. They had done the hard work of harvesting treasure for many years, and the Captain said it would almost be sinful not to rob those other pirates of their booty whenever we had the chance to do so. So instead of taking ships that plied the coast with scant treasure individually, we decided to masquerade as a merchant vessel to lure the coastal pirates to attack us. That way we could reverse our roles and do what we had done to the first pirate ship and village.

So our progress south was punctuated by our being raided by pirates whose ships we easily subdued and whose villages we overwhelmed and plundered afterwards. This way we amassed greater wealth by far than we had gathered during our time in the Canaries. In fact, we gathered so much gold and silver, jewels and ores that I wondered aloud whether it would be safe to travel with all that treasure.

The Captain had been thinking along the same lines, so we discussed strategy. We decided that we would have to plant some of our treasure ashore at the earliest opportunity in a place we would surely recognize after many years. We were flying Spanish colors now for disguise and convenience, and we came upon an anchorage crowded with ships with so many small boats rowing back and forth between those ships and the shore that it almost seemed American. We anchored a little farther out from the rest, and the Captain sent me ashore to discover the nature of the port.

I was disgusted to find that the rich port serviced the slave trade. Large holding pens held the slaves. The colony, which was designed especially for this kind of human trafficking, was larger than any of the villages we had encountered so far on our African journey.

Daily auctions of slaves were held in a public square with posts and chains to hold the slaves while the bidding took place. Slavers brought new slaves from the jungles, received their payments and then retreated to a religious house where they prayed.

While not impassable, the security for the slaves was certainly serious. Men with pistols, sabers and knives stood guard. Some of those were black. The slaves themselves were fed well and cleaned daily because the better they looked, the higher the prices they could command.

The trade was in gold and silver coins and bars, and I was impressed that the storehouse for the gold and silver seemed less well guarded than the slave pens. My mind immediately considered how the storehouse might be relieved of its contents during the night. The biggest constraint, it seemed to me, was the sheer weight of the potential plunder.

Coffee houses and trading posts had sprung up around the square with every conceivable African product from ivory tusks to hides of animals, spices of all kinds, and sacks of manioc roots and curious crystals.

A fortuneteller sold prophecies about the right and wrong days for purchases. Liquor, including rum, was available in bottles, casks and kegs, and a tavern sold African beverages that some said had been made from fermented grains. A row of small cabins was reserved for the sex trade, which was linked to the slave trade because the youngest and most beautiful of the female slaves were used there. Merchants could sample the wares for money before they purchased these slaves.

I was surprised to see that the slavers and the slave purchasers all used these slaves. I pretended that I was a potential customer, so I was shown to the amenities. I decided against participating when I saw how young the girl slaves were. When I emerged, I witnessed the public whipping of a very large black slave who had tried to escape. Evidently the stripes made by the whip were considered an adornment by potential buyers, who seemed not to regard the pain that was being inflicted on the slave.

I thought about that slave's desire to escape, and a vague plan began to form in my mind. I thought of the slaves as the means to get the gold and silver to the Sweet Cutlass. I thought that the best remuneration for their services would be their freedom. What would have to happen was a very rapid overcoming of all guards at the pens and the storehouse, a quick liberation of as many willing slaves as were necessary to carry the gold and silver to waiting boats that would row out to the Sweet Cutlass. I thought midnight would be the best time for executing this plan. I also thought some form of diversion would be necessary to keep the merchants busy while the treasure was removed. The anchored ships would be another problem—they were the greatest hazard to the welfare Sweet Cutlass unless, of course, some warships arrived unexpectedly.

On a whim I decided to visit the soothsayer's shop where fortunes were told. I was surprised to find that the soothsayer was a beautiful woman with green eyes and auburn hair. Without a word she took my hand and opened my palm, tracing my life line with her fingernail. She tried a half dozen languages until she hit upon English. Quickly with fire in her eyes, she said she had information that I must know and it would cost one piece of gold. I produced the gold coin, and she told me that a French warship would arrive early the next morning to receive the tribute that it collected once a month. She said the vessel stopped at all six slave ports—three to the north, this port, and two more ports to the south before the great diamond desert, so it would be laden with treasure when it arrived.

The soothsayer said she wanted me to spend the night with her for another gold coin, but I had now to get back to the Captain with the intelligence about the French ship.

I gave the woman a second gold coin and told her, "I'll return one day to spend the night with you." Her teeth were white, clean and even when she smiled.

She said, "Before you leave me, know that your lifeline suggests strength and a long life. I hope I'll see you again."

I replied, "You should be careful about the people to whom you sell your information. Informants are often killed for information far less important than what you've told me today."

"From your expression and the lines in your palm, I knew you would not kill me, not today anyway." With that enigmatical statement, she pushed me towards the door and said, "You have to run. There's not much time left to do what you have to do."

I returned to the whaleboat and had the coxswain row as fast as possible to the Sweet Cutlass where the Captain awaited my report. I arrived in the late afternoon, and the Captain and I spent a long while discussing what we should do. The Captain was very interested in the imminent arrival of the French warship, but he kept his mind focused on the gold and silver stream. When he had digested all the information I had gleaned, he asked me to bring the Second and Third Mates to his cabin for a conference. There the Captain outlined his plan of action, and it was better than anything I could have devised, though I had my doubts about the details of execution.

According to the Captain's plan, our crew would be divided into four teams, one led by the Captain and the other three led by us mates. We mates would strike that very midnight on the shore and at the anchorage while the Captain with a skeleton crew would sail out to meet the French warship.

So in the dark we mates shoved off in the whaleboat with six of the crew. We dropped the Second Mate off at the nearest merchant ship and then continued to shore where I showed the Third Mate where the storehouse was and told him and two men what they were to do as soon as possible after the explosion out on the water.

I instructed two hearties to seize and prepare two boats from the many on the beach for immediate departure when treasure arrived. I took the two remaining pirates with me to slit the throats of the guards and liberate the slaves from the pen.

My hearties and I had eliminated the guards at the pen when the explosion occurred on the merchant ship where the Second Mate had been dropped off. After that, the entire shore area came to life in a chaos of shouting and excitement. I opened the gate of the slave pen and motioned for the strongest male slaves to follow me to the storehouse, where the Third Mate and his men had already earned their share by killing the guardians of the gold and silver and found where the booty was hidden inside the enclosure.

The other slaves from the pen followed me and the slaves I had chosen, and a new idea occurred to me. In the storehouse, I passed out bags of gold and silver coins and bars of gold and silver to the slaves to carry down to the waterside where they were to put them in the two waiting boats. When all but a couple of bags remained in the storehouse, I threw their contents on the floor and motioned for the slaves to pick up what they could carry and run for the jungle. When they had scampered off in glee, I set fire to the storehouse and ran with the others to the whaleboat.

Setting out from the shore in the whaleboat with my men, I saw other men rowing towards the merchant ship that had suffered the explosion. At the same time, we were rowing as fast as possible out to the Sweet Cutlass. From the shore it would appear, I surmised, that the crews of ships that were farthest from shore were prudently returning to preserve their vessels. Looking back at the shore, I saw that by torchlight the denizens were scrambling to discover what had happened at the storehouse and at the pen. Some with torches had spread out looking for escaped slaves in the jungle. No one seemed to be interested in climbing into a boat to follow my crew.

We rowed and rowed, and ahead of the whaleboat appeared the Second Mate, swimming in the water and laughing his head off. I swung him aboard just in time before another great explosion rocked the merchant ship that the Second Mate had booby-trapped. The ship was riven by the blast and sank rapidly, while the rowboats that had tried to help looked on. Our three boats converged where the Sweet Cutlass should have been, but it had weighed anchor and was already proceeding to the north to intercept the French warship.

I signaled the other boats to pass leaders so that the three boats could proceed as a group in a line to the rear. We rowed in that line in the wake of the Sweet Cutlass. The wind was not strong, and our ship was undermanned without us. I looked for the Captain's sign at the rear of the ship, and I saw it bobbing up and down in the ship's wake. I ordered the boats to stroke harder, and I fished out the empty keg with the line attached. Hand over hand we pulled at the line while we continued to row towards the ship. I saw that on the starboard and port side lines were extended, and suddenly the great ship came about in a familiar maneuver. I signaled for the two boats to spread out to the right and left while the Sweet Cutlass continued to come about and then regained its course behind us. As the ship passed, the two boats and the whaleboat caught the lines extended to either side, and the transfer of the treasure and men began in earnest.

The gold and silver were hoisted aboard the Sweet Cutlass and taken immediately to the Captain's cabin. The slaves were told to lie on the deck by the mast, where they were provisioned with rum, apples and bread. When the two boats we had used for treasure and slaves had been emptied, they were abandoned to the open sea.

Meanwhile we in the whaleboat worked the davits and hauled the boat into place while the ship's watch team unfurled the sails. We all prepared to encounter the French warship. We sailed the rest of the night hugging the shore as much as possible, but we never found the French warship. Was the soothsayer's intelligence wrong?

The Captain laughed at the idea. He said that the French never could be on time for anything, even when gold and silver were at stake.

At dawn, the Captain told the helmsman to reverse course to the south again, and as the sun rose in the east over Africa the Captain went to his cabin to survey the piles of gold and silver bars, the thirty bags of coins and the six bags of uncut diamonds that had been taken in that one night.

The Captain resolved to take the course that the French warship was supposed to have taken and to visit the remaining two slave ports to the south to collect a similar booty. He advised us mates to look lively on watch and to brief the lookouts to be alert to sails on the horizon. We were now, he said, as much a rich prize as any he had ever taken. The Captain also had an idea about the slaves we had taken on board, and he asked me to help him communicate with them.

The slaves were glad to have been freed, but they were apprehensive about their future if they were set back on the shore. The one slave who could understand any language that we pirates knew was the huge black who had been whipped the day before. I explained to him that the Captain would put them all ashore if they liked. If that did not suit them, they had a choice that they must make at once. Either they became members of our crew, or they visited the sharks in the ocean.

The huge black man said a few words in the native Bantu language that all the slaves seemed to understand, and his fellow former slaves murmured among each other.

The huge man smiled and told me they were proud to join the Captain and his crew.

That is how the Sweet Cutlass gained ten of the fiercest fighters I have ever witnessed in a pirate crew. The former slaves adapted well to life at sea. They stood watches immediately under instruction and they learned fast. Our Third Mate became their leader, and I helped whenever special communication was necessary. Problems with morale were handled exclusively by the huge black man, who had a special regard among them. I later learned that he had been a chief among his own people, and it showed in his bearing and attitude.

The two slave ports to the south were much the same as the one we had raided with success. Our credibility among the slave traders was increased because of the presence of apparent slaves on our ship. We did not ask the slaves to go ashore to help us combat the slavers, but they volunteered for the job. They contended that their skills with language were superior to ours for the purpose. So when we struck at midnight on two occasions and opened the pens that held the slaves, our former slaves explained what was happening to the newly freed slaves. They also killed the slavers with such a vengeance that I could not withhold them from extending their retribution to the entire slaver community. We gained much gold and silver on both occasions, and we also gained twenty additional crew members, all former slaves. Because they could be trained by people they saw as their own extended family, the newbies learned quickly. None chose to live with the sharks.

So by the time we reached the Cape of Good Hope, we were a jolly ship unlike any other pirate vessel the world had known since ancient times. The Captain and crew were extremely happy that they had garnered a fortune from harvesting gold and silver; the former slaves were ecstatic that they had been freed and gone on to free others. The warm sentiments did not help much as we crossed under the Cape of Good Hope and ran through the rip tides and the cold winds that had blown many ships onto the inhospitable shore.

We soon plunged north and east along the east African shore towards Madagascar, and the Captain called for a meeting of us mates and the huge black we called Benjamin, who was chief of the former slaves now.

The Captain said that he had a plan that he hoped would satisfy everyone. He had two problems that needed to be solved, and the only way he knew to solve them both, he said, required the division of his crew into two parts, one part remaining on the Sweet Cutlass and the other part taking control of another ship of the same kind. In effect, he wanted to expand the piratical enterprise by fission and employ two ships working in tandem rather than one ship working alone. The Captain let his words sink in, and then he asked for comments from all of us.

I answered that the Captain's plan would probably work under conditions. First, the Captain would have to find an appropriate Captain for his second ship. Second, the Captain would have to determine how the two ships would operate together and share spoils. Third, the Captain would have to decide how to seize the ship that would be the Sweet Cutlass's companion.

The Second Mate then said that the crew now had natural divisions that were unique. By this, he meant that one portion of the crew understood only a foreign language and only one man could interpret for them. He implied that all the former slaves should be allocated to one ship instead of being distributed among the two vessels.

The Third Mate followed by stating that in any case additional crew members would be necessary to fill out the watch teams on both vessels. The most difficult decision—and it was the Captain's to make—was the fair apportionment of treasure according to pirate tradition since in the past the shares equaled the number of the surviving crew on one vessel. Would shares be according to vessel or according to the combination of vessels? The Third Mate suggested that if they could split into two crews, perhaps in future they could split again, so this fundamental determination had to be made right at the start so that feuding did not break out.

Benjamin, like the Captain, had listened carefully to everything that had been said. He asked the Captain's permission before he spoke, but when he spoke, he was direct and eloquent. First, he said, the First Mate was every bit ready for command of his own vessel, so the Captain's choice of a Captain for his companion ship was already made. Second, he said, the communication problem among former slaves was being solved through work since all of them knew their duties now and fit into the watch teams as they were. He said he could interpret as necessary for both ships. The man known as Reuben, who was Benjamin's second, could serve as his surrogate aboard the second vessel. Third, he said, the problems of recruitment would vanish if the Captain saw a way to increase his crews by freeing slaves just as he had already done. As for splitting treasure, what could be more valuable than freedom? The former slaves had already been given a priceless gift, and they were all very grateful. Benjamin said that the Captain would not only be the leader of his own ship, but the commander over both ships together.

Shares of all the treasure split across all the pirates would be most fair, but the Captain should have an additional share because of his dual role. Having said these things, Benjamin became quiet.

The Captain was lost in thought for a long while. When he shook his head and became conscious of his fellow pirates again, he said that they should share a few bottles of rum together. He extended that to the entire crew, and the ship was allowed to luff sail and rock in the ocean while everyone had his ration of rum, including the cabin boy and the lookouts that came down from the crow's nest. When the imbibition's had been taken, the Captain called for a meeting of all the crew at which he would make an announcement.

The Captain stood next to the steering wheel, and I stood by his side when he made his historic, game-changing speech, which was interpreted to the former slaves by Benjamin.

First, Captain Morgan thanked the crew for working well together and for earning more treasure in the last three raids than his ship had earned in its entire history.

He said, "Everyone aboard will share in the wealth in the pirates' fashion, with one share for each man regardless of origin, color or time in service." He hesitated for a moment to let that thought sink in. Hearing no objection, he pressed on.

The Captain continued, "I'm going to add a ship and split the crew between the two vessels so we can take twice the treasure in raids that can be coordinated. My current First Mate Abe will become the Captain of the second ship. Technically, the second ship as well as the Sweet Cutlass will still be under my command, though the second ship will have some measure of autonomy. The former slaves are now full partners in our pirate ventures. They'll be split evenly between the two ships, with Benjamin remaining on the Sweet

Cutlass. Benjamin will serve as interpreter for all the former slaves."

I saw that Benjamin swelled with pride upon hearing this news. The Captain had more to say.

"Shares will be treated on an equal basis across both ships with the entire crew of both ships sharing equally regardless of which ship had the most treasure to its credit. Any augmentations of the crew will be drawn from wherever seemed appropriate at the time, including other newly freed slaves."

The crew murmured in assent and smiled at this novel idea.

The Captain said, "I cannot well predict when all this will happen, but it will happen at the earliest opportunity and preferably before the ship ports in at Madagascar. I'll have other announcements in the coming weeks about who specifically will be allocated to each of the two ships when the time comes."

The Captain stopped and looked across his crew, taking the time to look each man directly in the eye. Then he ordered everyone to get back to their duty stations with the normal watch rotation. The stunned crew did as the Captain ordered.

During the ensuing weeks, the crew discussed the Captain's plan quietly among themselves. When the final lists were determined, the Third Mate and I were paired so that when I became Captain, he would become my First Mate. At the transition the Second Mate would become the Captain's new First Mate. I was proud of my new assignment but somewhat saddened that I would not be working directly by the Captain's side. I felt ready for my new role working in tandem with the Captain and crew of my former ship. Since the allocations had been determined, all the crew looked forward to our finding the ship that would be the Sweet Cutlass's complement.

We were nearing Madagascar when early one morning we espied what was probably a French-flagged vessel, with roughly the same size and rigging as the Sweet Cutlass. The Captain had examined the vessel through his spyglass for fully ten minutes before he passed the glass to me and asked me what I thought of the ship off the starboard quarter.

I liked what I saw and told the Captain it would do as the complement. With a nod the Captain directed a course to intercept, went to full sail and ordered the crew to prepare to board the ship.

It took eight hours to come within striking distance, and our initial volley was the wakeup call for our prey, which raised the Jolly Roger, came about and prepared to ram us. So the falsely flagged vessel was a pirate ship like ours, and now we were in a battle for our lives as well as our ship. The Captain took the Conn and ordered me to direct our fire on the closing vessel's masts. I ordered the batteries to fire at will, so smoke filled the air as the guns went off in a kind of rhythmic rotation.

Simultaneously, the Captain ordered the crew to man the port side and prepare to board with grappling hooks and lines. This confused our prey, which failed to understand the Captain's intentions. The pirate ship's Captain fully expected to ram us to starboard and to board on that side, but Captain Morgan was not an easy mark. In the final minutes, he ordered the Sweet Cutlass to come about to port, and the prey found itself unprepared for missing its ram and for a boarding in parallel to its starboard side from our port. For the Sweet Cutlass, this maneuver was our bread-and-butter signature move and a contributing factor to our success. We added to that surprise a massed boarding by a predominantly black boarding party, holding knives in their mouths and brandishing sabers. I shouted the guns to silence because in the melee that followed, I did not want friendly fire. The ships became bound by lines with grappling hooks, and now the joined vessels allowed free play of both crews across both decks. The Captain and I were in the thick of the fight, but I knew that the victor would be the crew whose Captain survived. So I ordered Benjamin to guard the Captain with his life, and I spirited myself over the side on a hanging line and raced through the fighting to the helm of our rival.

I did not wait for an invitation but pitched my knife so I held it by the blade. As quickly as I could, I hurled it fifteen feet into the heart of the rival pirate Captain. The man knew he was hit and the game was over, but the fight raged on. I shouted to Captain Morgan that his rival was dead. I noticed that Benjamin was taking down two assailants who had been trying to kill my Captain. Now Benjamin raised both arms and in a terrible, booming voice said something in his native language. The former slaves stood back from their work for a moment to allow their adversaries to hear what Captain Morgan was saying.

The Captain sharply ordered everyone on both ships to lower their weapons because he had an offer for all ears. All pirates from both ships stopped fighting to listen.

Captain Morgan announced, "My worthy rival has been killed." He gestured towards me, and I pointed to the place where that dead Captain lay.

After we had paused to let everyone consider what we had revealed, the Captain announced, "I intend to combine the treasure and the surviving crew members of both ships in a single venture, with no prejudice whatsoever. Any pirate who objects to this proposal will be killed immediately and fed to the sharks. All who agree to join me will be given a place in the new crews befitting his current role. I'll count to three to hear an objection, and if none is forthcoming, everyone will drop his weapons on the decks and await further instructions."

The Captain did not have to reach the count of three when weapons began to fall on the decks of both ships. Benjamin then ordered the ex-slaves to pick up all weapons and place them before the mast of the Sweet Cutlass. The Captain ordered the crews of both ships to muster before their respective masts. He ordered those of his own crew who had been designated as members of the complementary ship to gather their belongings and proceed to their new vessel. He told me to take charge of my new command, and I gladly did so.

When I was ready I asked the three mates of the captured ship to stand forward. The First Mate I offered the position of Second Mate under my command. When he appeared to be reluctant, I drew my pistol and shot him in the head. I then offered the position to the Second Mate, who eagerly agreed to serve. I offered the position of Third Mate to the current Third Mate of the captured vessel, and he also agreed to serve without cavil. I ordered the Second Mate to identify half of the captured crew to ship aboard the Sweet Cutlass within the next ten minutes. I told my First Mate to see that the division was carried out and the identified men left the ship with their belongings and joined the crew of the Sweet Cutlass.

Within ten minutes the transfer had been completed. I ordered my First Mate to sort out and set the evening watch and to clear the decks of the dead and the wounded. Anyone wounded too severely to serve was to be given the coup de grace and hurled overboard with the other dead. I told my First Mate to repair the damaged rigging and await the order to move ahead based on Captain Morgan's orders. When the

First Mate told me he was ready, I called over to Captain Morgan that I was ready to separate ships and proceed after him.

Captain Morgan asked me, "Captain Abe, what are you going to call your new vessel?"

I had thought about this for as long as I knew I was going to have my own command. Without hesitation I told him, "Night Lightning."

At this name he laughed deep and long. He then ordered his men to cut all binding ties between the Sweet Cutlass and the Night Lightning, set the evening watch and unfurl all sails. I did the same, and when the Sweet Cutlass pulled ahead into the night, I saw the light on its fantail and ordered my helmsman to follow it.

Satisfied that the Night Lightning was on the right course with the watch set, I proceeded to the dead Captain's cabin and there found silver and gold, charts and maps marked with the location of buried treasure. Hiding in the closet was the former Captain's cabin boy with blue eyes and straw blonde hair. I smiled to show him he had nothing to fear.

"You have a new master. Fetch me a bottle of rum."

The boy did gladly fetch one from a store of bottles and kegs in a special compartment in the Captain's cabin. The boy spoke a little English along with his French, so I thought we would get along just fine.

"I know the places where the best ladies live in Madagascar. They are very good in bed, but they know everyone and everything that is going on in east Africa."

I knew I had found a treasure beyond comparison. I told him, "You are now the Captain's cabin boy for the Night Lightning."

He liked the new name for the ship and repeated it to himself so that he would remember it. By the time the First

Mate had come to report the ship's status, the boy was asleep in his cot.

My First Mate told me that all was well. He said he would shadow the midwatch, and I told him I would shadow afterward until the morning watch. I showed the First Mate some of the gold and silver pelf that had been hidden in the cabin, but I did not mention the charts and maps I had found with the locations for treasure clearly marked on them. I realized that I was already learning the prerogatives of being a ship's Captain.

The next morning's sunrise was resplendent. A pair of whales swam alongside the ship as if they were traveling in company. The only other ship on the horizon was the Sweet Cutlass dead ahead. The crew mustered after their morning meal, and I said a few words indicating that we should be ready for action at an instant's notice. I ordered a meeting of the mates by the helm to discuss the plan for the day, and they went below on the weather decks to tell the men what I had said in their own ways.

When they had finished and the men were at their assigned duties, the Second Mate and Third Mate came to see me as much to gauge their new Captain as to be sure I knew of their loyalty to me.

I looked each one in the eyes before speaking. "I don't care whether you like me or not. I intend to increase the wealth of all the crew through our common labor, but I also demand of every hearty his total effort to make us a success. Anyone not doing his utmost will be liable to the lash or worse instantly, and that applies to mates as well as ordinary crew. Choose others who can succeed you if either of you should die in battle. Give me your prospective replacements' names by the end of the afternoon watch." I spoke with authority, and the men seemed to respond favorably to my clarity.

Seeing them off, I retreated to the Captain's cabin and reviewed the Captain's log. I drew a line under the last entry that the former Captain made, and I wrote my initial notations in that log. I had just completed my entry when I heard a commotion at my door. The First Mate entered my room to say that the lookout in the crow's nest had sighted a warship on the horizon abaft the port beam with constant bearing, decreasing range. I gave the order for the crew to take their battle stations, and I was very glad we had missed the main brace in our boarding exercise on the previous day.

Both our ships were flying false French colors when the English warship came into close visual range. My men stood by their cannons ready to fire, and the crew lined the port side ready for action as well.

The English ship fell slowly behind the Night Lightning, and I waited for any sign of hostile action from our rear. The wind gave my ship the advantage if the English ship chose to attack, and I wondered why its Captain had so insistently closed as if my ship were his target and then decided to pass astern. I thought it must be clear to the Englishman that we were travelling in company with the ship ahead. By closing on my ship, it had perhaps missed the identity of the Sweet Cutlass entirely.

Perhaps, I reasoned, the English ship was looking for some other vessel sailing these waters. The ship passed astern without any sudden threatening maneuvers, and then it continued on a track orthogonal to ours until it was far too distant for any action against us. I consequently ordered my crew to stand down from their battle stations and to set the normal sailing watch again.

We followed the Sweet Cutlass to a small cove off the west coast of Madagascar and we dropped anchors there. Captain Morgan called for a gam, so we met in between our anchored vessels in our whaleboats where we talked about what to do with our combined treasures. We decided that we would take a portion of our pelf from both ships and bury it at a place in this cove that we could relocate easily. I mentioned to Captain Morgan that just such a place had been indicated on a map among the personal belongings of the departed Captain of my new ship. The Captain affected not to have heard what I told him. I was not surprised that he might be jealous of my discovery. He said we would gather our treasures into two chests and proceed separately in our whaleboats to a point just outside the view of the anchorage. We were to arrive there at an hour before sundown accompanied by one expendable person and a coxswain each.

I knew the drill from long experience, and I selected one of the surlier of the captured crew members as my expendable person. He helped me lower my chest of treasure into my whaleboat and rowed around the point of land that put us out of view of the anchored ships.

Captain Morgan's whaleboat had preceded us, and the Captain and his man were already ashore while his coxswain waited patiently by the whaleboat for their return.

My own whaleboat made land beside the other, and my man and I carried the chest and a shovel inland after the Captain and his man. We all arrived at a place where an ancient tree hung over an enormous rock. There Captain Morgan placed the heel of his right boot against a slot in the rock, and he marched thirty paces directly to the east. There he threw down the shovel he was carrying and told his man to dig.

I did the same and ordered my man to help dig with the man the Captain brought with him. Captain Morgan then He brought out a bottle of rum and invited me to drink with him. We drank together while our men dug, and we had nearly finished the bottle of rum when my man struck something hard and the two men scrambled to unearth what lay below.

My man brought up a skull and what looked like a femur. He showed them to me, and I nodded. Captain Morgan nodded also.

Captain Morgan's man then split the skull of my man with his shovel and pulled his lifeless body next to the hole they had excavated together. He placed the two chests side by side at the bottom of the hole and was about to begin filling the hole with dirt when I cocked my pistol and shot him through the heart.

I heaved his body into the pit and placed it on one side of the chests. I pulled my own man's body into the pit and placed it on the other side of the chests. Draining the last of my rum, I threw the bottle into the pit. With one shovel I worked to fill the hole, and soon Captain Morgan was helping me fill it with the other shovel. We worked rapidly, and soon we were smoothing the surface to remove any indication that the earth had been disturbed that evening.

When we satisfied ourselves that our work would not be detected, we laid some foliage over the area and retreated to our whaleboats where in semi-darkness our coxswains awaited us. Separately we were rowed back to our ships, guided by lights we had ordered to be lit on board at sunset.

Before I retired in my cabin, I consulted the map that showed where treasure was buried to verify that the site where Captain Morgan and I had buried our own treasure had the same location on the map as the mark that had been made on it. I wondered at that coincidence and recalled that

Captain Morgan had affected not to hear me when I had mentioned the map earlier that day. Was the map somehow connected to Captain Morgan's prior exploits in this area of the world? Was the location where we buried our treasure the repository of other chests like the ones we buried this afternoon? I made a few notes on the edges of the map and hid it among my belongings in my cabin. I then ordered my cabin boy to bring me another bottle of rum.

He mentioned that some of the gold and silver had disappeared from the cabin and that a small chest was also missing. I told him that I had noticed that also. I was mightily pleased that my cabin boy was so attentive.

He rejoined that he had overheard two of the crew talking by the apple barrel. They muttered among themselves that a man had accompanied the Captain ashore in the whaleboat but the man had not returned. One said that he was glad the man had not come back because he was a very bad man, always finding fault even when a job was done well. I was curious about how the crew was reacting to my decisions, but I wanted to exude confidence.

I waited for the boy to say more, but the boy had nothing more to say on that account. He asked me whether he could do me another service that night.

"Not now, so get some sleep. Tomorrow will be a busy day."

As the boy settled into his cot for the night, I sipped my rum and brooded over what had happened to bring me to this strange place and to grant my wish of one day becoming the Captain of my own ship.

After midnight I wandered out of my cabin and walked the deck of my own ship. A late night watch stander bid me adieu. We looked out over the still bay water together at the other ship at anchor there, the Sweet Cutlass, with the orange flame of its stern lamp barely visible. The watch stander smoked a shank of hemp and invited me to look at the stars with him. He said the stars had brought us here. I thought he had a point.

Chapter Five
Pirates of Zanzibar

anchored the Night Lightning off the main port city of the island of Zanzibar, in water so pellucid you could watch fish and crabs active right to the sandy bottom five fathoms below. The Sweet Cutlass was anchored a small distance away. Both ships had spent the last two weeks doing repairs and provisioning after a most profitable sail north from Madagascar. We had raided merchants of all flags along the way north: British, Portuguese, French and American. As we sailed in the ocean to the east of the island we increasingly took merchants from Yemen and Oman because the spices and slaves of Zanzibar supplied all the vast desert lands of Arabia. Captain Morgan had rightly figured that our most profitable ventures since we left the Canaries were those tied to the slave trade, so he wanted to see what might be plundered in the waters surrounding Zanzibar, the capital of the slave trafficking enterprise in this part of the world.

Now our ship's holds were filled to the brim with gold, silver, jewels, ivory tusks, animal hides, exotic fabrics and bags of rich spices. Several of the hearties had animal pets like monkeys that ran about the decks and colorful birds that sat on shoulders or flew up to perch in the rigging. The animals and birds had been taken in our recent raids. Captain Morgan and I had found several small, deserted islands in the channel to the west of the main island where we surreptitiously buried a large part of our gold and silver in the usual way. We still kept aside enough of our hoard to distribute small bags of coins to each of our hearties to spend in the old stone city as they liked.

Before the crew went ashore, we warned them that the Islamic law of the land made our usual carousing, brawling and bullying dangerous to life and limb. While in the stone city we witnessed public beheadings for murderers and chopping off of hands of thieves. We also witnessed more slaves than we ever thought possible in pens and in chains. The slavers were a devilish lot with swords, knives, prods and whips. Though Benjamin was incensed and wanted to free the slaves, Captain Morgan managed to restrain him.

The British, he explained patiently, were trying to eradicate the trade throughout the world, but it would be hard going. Zanzibar's entire good fortune depended on the slave trade, so it would take at least two centuries, maybe more, to stamp out the trafficking entirely. The massive fort on the island was stocked with troops who had modern weapons. We gauged assault too risky for us, and we resolved to save our piracy for our familiar ocean setting.

Ashore, Benjamin and the other former slaves posed as our slaves dressed in fine robes and fancy turbans that we had seized from the merchants we had pirated. I admit that we made a colorful parade when we wandered through the streets and market places. We all wore silk in all colors, exotic feathers, turbans and hides of wild animals. Benjamin's parrot perched on his massive shoulder speaking pirate code to all passersby, "Avast, ye lubbers!" being his favorite cry. Behind Captain Morgan and I ranged a long line of "slaves" to bear the provisions that we bought in the markets. When the muezzins climbed into their minarets to call the people to prayer and the religious police roamed the streets looking for slackers, we and our retinue sought refuge in a spacious house that Captain Morgan knew from his former adventures.

The house was near the center of the city. It had high walls like a fortress and no windows. In the center of the walled grounds was a magnificent, square garden with fountains and plants in which colorful songbirds played. Along all sides of this central garden were two score rooms. Beautiful ladies in silk sat outside these rooms and waited for companions to bargain and then go inside the rooms with them. Liquor was available by the bottle or cask. Our crew either went into the rooms with the ladies or sat drinking at tables on chairs under the shade of lemon and orange trees covered with fruits. The whole impression was of an outdoor bacchanal. We Captains sat at a special table on a veranda above one of the rooms, where the woman named Alia who presided over the house catered to our every whim. The woman knew that she would be richly rewarded for the information she imparted.

Alia told us that a great commotion had erupted when two pirate ships began marauding merchant vessels on the rich trade route between Zanzibar and Arabia. The Englishmen and Americans had separately met with the Sultan of Zanzibar to offer their warships' services to rid the seas of the pirate menace. Alia said that the sultan was not perturbed. Her spies reported that the sultan had laughed at the foreigners' concern. He then told them that everything was in Allah's capable hands. As far as the sultan was concerned, trade on Zanzibar was his concern. What happened to the ships that came to or went from the island was decidedly not his concern. As long as the spices, ivory and slaves kept coming from the mainland of Africa, and as long as they were traded for gold, silver, jewels and silk in his bazaars, he was satisfied.

If Arabia wanted to protect their ships, they could do so on their own. The sultan suggested that the best way to deal with pirates was to use other pirates against them. He then regaled his concerned visitors with stories from the fabled One Thousand and One Nights of Queen Scheherazade until they tired and went away frustrated.

Captain Morgan and I knew that the English and American warships would try to attack us no matter what the sultan thought. We did not know what to make of the threat from warships of Arabia because we knew of no such vessels.

While Captain Morgan went below to have Alia entertain him specially, I drank my rum and observed the crew enjoying themselves as they drank, joked and whored. Soon enough the hearties would be climbing into the rigging of the ships and preparing to board the merchantmen that were our prey at the risk of their lives and limbs. Why should they not enjoy to the limit the life of a pirate ashore, when tomorrow they might be visiting Davy Jones' locker in the cerulean sea?

After a long interval, the Captain emerged looking refreshed and robust with Alia smiling and following behind him while adjusting her robe. I rose and whistled loud and long to alert the crew that our business here should be brought to an end. The crew mustered by the exit so that we could count them all, and we processed back into the street outside the house and made our way back to our landing in the port where the whaleboats took the hearties in batches back to the ships.

As was our custom, Captain Morgan was among those who manned the first whaleboat to depart, and I was among those who manned the last whaleboat from the shore. That way, one Captain was available on land and the other at sea until all the hearties were safely back on board. I kept the best fighters with me for that final boat because the fewer we were with evening fast approaching, the more vulnerable we became. It was a good thing that I was prudent that day because a rowdy group of sailors, returning from the stone city to their own ship, decided to pick a fight with us for no better reason than their own hubris.

The fight started with name-calling and progressed rapidly to shoving and fisticuffs. Then one of the other ship's crew drew a knife. I could not believe their audacity. Could they not see that my hearties were battle-hardened veterans who loved a fight? My men drew their weapons and flew in a frenzy to kill their enemies. In short order my men dispatched the other crew to the last man. They were wiping their blades or picking over the corpses when we were espied and the alarm was raised. I did not wait for our own whaleboat to return, but ordered my men to seize the whaleboat that the now-deceased crew had intended to use. We pulled away from shore just as the first troops became visible with their torches lit over the hill. My hearties pulled with all their strength.

I lit a torch and held it high to make us a clear target for the pursuing troops. I commanded my hearties to row for the nearest ship in the anchorage and ignore what was happening on shore. From the shore, I guessed it appeared that the whaleboat we had commandeered belonged to the nearest ship out. I could see from the motions and hear from the shouting that the troops, whose numbers were increasing, were preparing to launch boats in pursuit of us, the presumed murderers. I steered the whaleboat to that nearest ship, but when we arrived there, I doused my torch and urged the men to pull around the ship and head in darkness for the Night

Lightning as if their lives depended on their efforts. I was not worried for myself but for our ships. Much depended on our coordination in the darkness.

From their own torches, I observed that the three boats that had pulled out from shore were crammed with troops. The pursuing boats would surely continue on their headings to the ship we had now left behind.

By the time we reached our own rightful ship, we would have to act fast to weigh anchor because the troops would know their mistake and might be coming after us next. I saw ahead our own whaleboat from the Night Lightning rowing to shore to pick us up, but I managed to get the attention of the coxswain and had it come alongside.

I transferred half of my hearties to the other whaleboat and ordered them to row fast to the Sweet Cutlass and tell Captain Morgan to weigh anchor and set sail. We would rendezvous at dawn or just after off the small island just around the tip of Zanzibar.

So now two boatloads of desperate men were making for our two ships. When the boats arrived, the whole crews of each ship were given orders to get underway at once. It was a close thing, but the ships managed to unfurl sail and catch the light breeze in every inch of sail surface before the deceived troops could gain their bearings and follow us.

I was much relieved that we would make it out alive. It had been a close thing, but I actually enjoyed the feeling that for a while our lives had hung in the balance.

The next morning at the planned rendezvous, my hearties that had jumped into the Sweet Cutlass's whaleboat were returned to the Night Lightning.

Captain Morgan and I had a gam at which I told him my version of what had happened the previous night at the landing. We realized that the chances that warships would be sent out to pursue us were scant. No one who had witnessed the killings aside from our crews remained alive. Who would the authorities blame for the slaughter now that hot pursuit had failed?

Captain Morgan considered this matter as we both had another swallow of rum, and he said that it was high time we got back to our business of piracy. Knowing from Alia how the sultan thought about depredations at sea, we decided that the Night Lightning should proceed up the west coast of the island and take whatever prey it could find there while the Sweet Cutlass proceeded up the east coast of Zanzibar and preyed upon the merchant shipping there. I said that the Night Lightning would take what it could in the Zanzibar Channel for the next fortnight and then swing north around the island and meet the Sweet Cutlass one day's sail due east of Zanzibar five days after breaking off from the Channel. We drank to that idea and returned to our separate ships to execute our plan.

The Zanzibar Channel has thick traffic, so we had our choice of target vessels. At first, we avoided ships that came from Africa and instead focused on ships that were returning from Zanzibar having traded there. We took a ship each day for sixteen days, careful to kill all aboard and to send the ships we captured with their lifeless crews to Davy Jones. I then decided that I would switch tactics and concentrate on vessels that came from Africa. I did not want to take ships that were transporting slaves, but every ship had some slaves as cargo. In seven days we harvested ten ships, sparing only the slaves, which we freed and allowed to sleep on our weather decks. I did not know at the time what I was going to do with the newly-freed slaves, but the answer came in a wondrous way.

An English merchant ship closed on the Night Lightning on the last day before we had planned to desist our pirate adventure and turn north. I ordered my hearties to prepare for action, but I saw that the merchant was unarmed with what appeared to be slaves on its weather decks.

Because of the English animadversion to slavery, I was curious why the ship carried so many slaves out in the open. I called for a gam with the Captain of that ship, and we met in our whaleboats between our two vessels. The merchant Captain informed me that his mission was to buy as many slaves as he could find and free them. A wealthy, religious philanthropist had discovered the funds to pay for the men's freedom.

I could not believe my luck—or the luck of my newly freed slaves. I told the Captain that I had sixty slaves on my weather decks that I could immediately transfer to his ship if he would take them aboard. He said he would take all the slaves I could give him, and he remarked that I had what appeared to be slaves working as part of my crew. I told him that I had personally freed and trained those men to be my crew and that they had an equal share in everything my crew did. The Captain, who was a devout man, said, "The Lord's Name be praised!"

So the Captain returned to his ship and fetched bags of gold and silver to pay for the slaves I had already freed. I was astonished at the amount he was willing to pay for those slaves. When I received his payment, I ordered my crew to help ferry the sixty freed slaves in batches. So the sixty freed slaves were transported off our decks working the two ships' whaleboats to take them from the Night Lightning to the English merchant. When the entire transaction had been completed, I realized that trafficking slaves to freedom could be very profitable business. I was not the only pirate who realized this, as I soon learned.

After the last slave had been transported from my ship, my lookout shouted from the crow's nest that a ship was fast approaching from the south with constant bearing and decreasing range. As a precaution I ordered my crew to their battle stations. I noticed that the English merchant that had taken aboard our purchased slaves was making rapid preparations to flee to the north.

To my surprise, the English merchant seemed to be fleeing the same approaching ship we had sighted. Through my spyglass I saw the telltale signs that the approaching vessel was a pirate ship flying the Jolly Roger. It was making significant headway and its men were poised to board. I had never seen a ship whose decks were arrayed like this one. I saw chains all over its decks and bales of rope. The ship paid the Night Lightning no heed whatsoever as it passed but kept its sights on the English merchant ship. I surmised the game in an instant: this pirate was preying upon the ship that paid gold at sea to free slaves because it could take both the slaves and the gold and sell the freed slaves to the highest bidder ashore.

I had no stake in the one-sided fight that was going to take place between that lone pirate vessel and the unarmed English merchant with the freed slaves aboard it, but I reasoned that the profitable business of freeing slaves could only continue if it was protected. Besides, protecting my future investment was good business.

In any case, it seemed a good idea at the time for the Night Lightning to blow that pursuing pirate vessel out of the water. The ship went to full sail with a course to intercept the vessel we were now pursuing. The batteries prepared to take out the mainmast and main brace with a concentrated volley at my command. The Jolly Roger ran up the mast. The Night Lightning picked up speed and closed on the pirate ship from its starboard quarter. I ordered my men to prepare to board to port.

At the right time when in the foaming wake of the pirate ship, I ordered the helm to the right and ordered the batteries to fire. In a moment, the main rigging of the pirate ahead fell in a thousand splinters that flew like spears through the bodies of the pirates on its decks. The helm came left and the crew prepared to use grappling hooks.

As the Night Lightning came alongside the pirate ship, I ordered luff sail and the boarding. So over the side went the grappling hooks and their lines with the hearties binding the lines fast and rushing across to the enemy's decks, slashing and piercing as they raged.

The English merchant continued sailing north while my hearties cut down the pirates to the last man. I ordered my men to search the ship's hold for valuables and hoist them over to the Night Lightning. I left the ship in the care of my First Mate and climbed aboard the prize. I went straight to the pirate Captain's cabin and found enough treasure, papers and logs to fill many sacks, which my hearties conveyed back to my own cabin aboard the Night Lightning.

In the hold of the pirate ship, my men discovered in shackles one hundred and twenty malnourished slaves who could barely walk. They also found one hundred elephant tusks, huge stacks of animal hides, and spices in great burlap bags, barrels of malmsey and kegs of gunpowder. All these we transferred to the Night Lightning, the slaves unshackled and left to sit and sleep on the weather decks with sufficient food and water for them all. When the entire pirate's pelf had been shifted to my vessel, the pirate ship was scuttled and cut free.

The Jolly Roger was struck on Night Lightning and the French ensign flown astern. The Night Lightning then moved ahead to the north at increasing speed while the pirate ship and its dead crew sank behind us slowly beneath the undulating waves. I ordered the helmsman to steer with constant bearing on the English merchant ship, which had slowed when it realized the pirate vessel was no longer in pursuit.

We overtook the English merchant, and I asked its Captain for another gam. It took the man some time to decide to meet me because he now knew that I captained a pirate vessel, but we did meet in our respective whaleboats. I told him that we had taken on board one hundred twenty emaciated slaves that had been held by the pirate ship. These slaves had been freed by me and now needed immediate attention. I asked whether the English merchant ship could accommodate them all and give them what they needed.

The Captain said he could probably take all of the additional slaves aboard as long as they would stay on the weather decks. He confirmed he would pay the same amount per man as he had for the former sixty that he had received earlier in the day. I told him we had a deal, and we made the exchange before sundown. On parting, the Captain asked me whether I could work with him to free the slaves at the same rate per slave as we had agreed to. I told him that might be possible, but I had to confer with my partners before I made a firm decision. If I could do business with him, I said, I would be back and find him.

After that the English merchant steered north again and the Night Lightning steered northeast on a course to clear the north of Zanzibar before it turned east-southeast so as to meet the Sweet Cutlass at the rendezvous as planned. That night my First Mate came to my cabin to discuss what we had done during the day. He was frankly amused by the turn of events.

"Captain, today we decided to sell sixty freed slaves to a person who was alleged not to be in the slave trade. Then we captured and scuttled a pirate ship with twice as many slaves in its hold, and we sold those to the Englishman at the same rate. Finally, we considered making the liberation of slaves a major business venture in the Zanzibar Channel." He laughed at the idea of pirates becoming altruists.

"I admit I find the idea ironical, but let's go through the numbers together. We earned significant wealth in gold and silver coins for selling one hundred and eighty men into freedom. In addition to those profits, we seized from the adversary pirate ship spoils that add up to another small fortune that all aboard will share. We lost no men during the last fourteen days, which is itself a marvel. We have the option never to return if we find that ordinary piracy is for any mix of reasons a more attractive course to continue. First Mate, what would you have done if you had been in command of the Night Lightning during the last few days?"

The First Mate brooded on that question, and then he said, "My problem is that I would never have been able to think things through in one tenth of the time that you did. I wonder whether I ever could be intelligent enough to be a successful Captain."

He was a proud man, so this admission came with some difficulty for him.

I told him, "I once had doubts about becoming Captain of a ship, and that was a good thing for me. Captain Morgan still has more tricks up his sleeve than I know, and I learn something new from him every time we work together. I hope you'll tell me when you think you have better ideas than mine. I'll listen carefully to your recommendations, but I'll make the decisions as long as I am Captain. I'll not unilaterally make the decision to continue liberating slaves as a business. Two things bother me about that."

I had the First Mate's full attention now.

"I am worried that pirates just like the scum that we killed this day will be a threat to the liberators as long as slavery is managed on a large scale. I'm also worried that men less scrupulous than the good English Captain to whom we sold slaves today might take his place. That would mean the slaves we sold might be resold right back into slavery by the people we sold them to. Finally, the more successful the liberators are, the more likely the Sultan of Zanzibar is to reconsider his position about securing the sea lines of control on both sides of the island. After all, he has the English and the Americans lobbying him vehemently to engage us pirates with their warships."

The First Mate then told me with fire in his eyes, "I'd rather be a pirate than a slave. I hate slavery and everyone involved in the trade with every ounce of my being."

I uncorked a bottle of rum and passed it to him with a gesture to drink. He did so gratefully and passed the bottle back to me so I could join him.

When I had drunk a long swallow, I told him, "I share your hatred of the slave trade, and if it were in my power I would find a way to free all slaves. I discussed the matter with Captain Morgan, and we agreed that is a bridge too far. Slavery has been around since the beginnings of humankind. I advise you to think instead of what we can do to maximize crew share by whatever we did. If in the process of piracy we can seize coins and liberate slaves, so much the better for us and the slaves."

The First Mate seemed to be satisfied with that approach.

I asked my First Mate, "How do the former slaves among our crew feel about freeing other slaves?"

The First Mate knit his brows and said, "The former slaves are extremely gratified at what we did to free the other slaves. They're proud to have had a part in that action. I cannot be sure, but I think they would be proud to die in the process of liberating slaves. One former slave talked about going back to his home village. Slave traders had burned his village to the ground and killed everyone they did not take as a slave. The former slave told me the Night Lightning was now as close to a home that he had ever known. He was glad to be part of the crew. The man said he had no family and no friends except for those he fights alongside. I told him that he was thinking like most pirates everywhere."

On that note, the First Mate went to relieve the watch. I reflected on Captain Morgan's wisdom in sparing this man from being fed to sharks and shook my head. It was certainly true that I learned continually from my mentor, and now I was learning from my protégé also.

As we passed around Zanzibar and intersected the sea lines that extended invisibly in all directions, I kept the crew on their normal watch standing routines and ordered the mates to keep the men active cleaning ship and cutting mare's tails and doing all the tedious daily tasks of sailors everywhere. I had the First Mate organize knot tying exercises and drills. Once the men had furled the sails and while the ship rose and fell dead in the water, I told the First Mate to take the Conn and plunged into the sea. Treading water, I asked everyone else who could swim to follow me. Around half the crew plunged in, and we swam around the ship four times before we climbed up the knotted ropes to the decks again and dried ourselves in the sunshine.

Another time, I organized a contest to see which hearty could climb to the crow's nest fastest. I also encouraged competition in knife throwing and swordsmanship. I had already told each mate to find a man to train as his replacement, and now I rotated those replacements in the watch routine and had the mates perform over watch to see how they did and what they needed to learn.

We made good time, and one day out from due east of the old stone city of Zanzibar, my lookout sang out, "Sail ahoy!."

I answered, "Where away?"

"On the horizon, one point abaft the starboard bow."

There with my spyglass I saw a sail and surmised it must be from the Sweet Cutlass. I ordered the helmsman to keep a constant bearing on that ship as we closed.

In fact, we did not close because the ship was sailing at full speed to the east. I therefore ordered full sail and increased our speed therefore to the maximum. I ordered extra sail too, and we began to close with the target vessel gradually, but it was clear to me that we would not close until well after dark. This was not good because from the south we saw a storm advancing rapidly, and the rains from such storms in these climes came in a deluge in which a ship could become lost. The winds picked up and the storm's effects began to buffet us, so I took up sail and sacrificed speed for stability and safety.

My tactics changed from overtaking the vessel ahead to surviving the onslaught of the storm. That was prudent because the lightning flashed and the thunder roared as if Hades had opened. The sea state rose with cat's paws and then great waves with spindrift. On the southern horizon under the huge black canopy that was rapidly covering the skies danced wispy waterspouts. I could see a wall of rain approaching, but I could do nothing about it except to have my watch standers tie themselves in place with line and keep movements about the decks to a minimum.

When the rain hit us, it came in sheets and then in a continuous torrent. The sea beneath us boiled with waves and winds, and I ordered the helmsman to change the ship's heading directly into the storm so we met each wave head-on rather than side-on. That way we would not capsize, but the seawater swept over the ship from stem to stern and the undulating waves made the oak of the ship groan under stress.

I held myself in place with a rope, and I had tied the helmsman in place with a rope as well. We two looked into the jaws of the storm together, and the helmsman looked up at me as if I as Captain had some power over the elements that would save us all. Alas, I had no such power, though the respect in my helmsman's eyes was palpable. I watched carefully as the ship was tossed about for anything that we could do to mitigate the storm's effects. There was precious little we could do. It hardly mattered to my crew that I had seen such storms along the Virginia coast in America and in the Caribbean.

What did they care about other storms when this was the storm that might hurl us down to Davy Jones where we would have all the treasure in the world, though we would have no way to spend it? Everyone on board was soaked wet to the bone, and seawater was so thick as we passed through waves that it seemed we would be swallowed up. Everything not tied down washed overboard.

The thunder and lightning kept booming and crackling through the night, and the horrific wind whistled in the rigging like the cry of a Banshee. My helmsman at one point said he saw the kraken looming up from the waves ahead, but then the apparition was gone. Except when the lightning flashed, we were sailing blind.

The ship was well named this night, I thought, since when the lightning flashed, the ship was still there, even if it was partially under seawater that fell off both sides of the decks in great streams as the ship was lifted to the top of the next wave and then dropped into the trough again.

I do not know how we managed to survive that ordeal, but sometime after midnight or thereabouts, the rain stopped completely, and the wind subsided along with the thunder and lightning receding behind the ship. The sea still swelled and fell more than normal, but the clouds raced away to the north.

Finally the ocean lay almost flat and the gibbous moon shone through the breaking clouds. I ordered the helmsman to steer in parallel with the waves now because it was safe to do so. I asked the bo'sun of the watch to tally the watch standers. He did so and reported that all remained on station. No hearty had been lost to the storm. I ordered the watch to be shifted, and the men emerged to take their places and relieve the watch standers who had braved the elements.

By sunrise, when the sea was flat as a board, the clouds were gone and a light zephyr blew from the west, the ship glistened as if it had been cleansed. The crew went about the decks checking for damage and tidying up. One hearty brought me a strange fish that had landed on the deck. I had never seen it's like before, but I ordered it scaled, cleaned and chopped into fish stew.

We were not becalmed, and humidity was considerably reduced, so I ordered all hands to be watchful for signs of the Sweet Cutlass. We were now a day late for our rendezvous, and no one could say where we were ourselves located now that the storm had passed. I reasoned that going towards the rising sun was as good a direction as any. So we edged towards the far horizon waiting for a sign.

It was noon around watch change when we had our first indication that our heading was correct. We fished out of the water a piece of wood that I knew well, because in it I had once carved the name Sweet Cutlass. It was the stern piece from the whaleboat of my former ship, and it did not bode well for the ship and crew. I ordered an expanding square search around the place where we had found the flotsam.

I dropped an empty keg in the water so we would have a reference, and we kept expanding our search around that keg looking for other remains of the Sweet Cutlass. We also kept our eyes peeled for signs of a sail on the horizon. By nightfall we had achieved no results, and I began to fear that the worst had befallen the Sweet Cutlass. I considered the irony that a pirate ship that had sailed unvanquished for years finally succumbed to a ferocious storm in the Indian Ocean.

I had visions of Captain Morgan regaling Davy Jones and sharing a bottle of rum with the vast treasure of the deep extending in all directions. The Captain Morgan I imagined had a bloated face, and his hair rose up and down in the depths, but his smile was that knowing, half-malicious smile that meant, "Arrgh!" Since the night was likely to be calm and since we had nowhere to go immediately, I ordered the sails to be luffed and the crew to rest on station when they were below decks or on watch. It was a long night of reflection for every hearty.

The next morning, I mustered the crew before the mast.

"Men, we don't know for certain that the Sweet Cutlass went down in the storm, but we have the evidence of the stern piece of its whaleboat to indicate that at least it suffered great damage. Because we don't know the ship's fate, we can't mourn its loss. But we can't waste more time looking for what might never be found. We'll be returning to the waters near Zanzibar to do what we always have done—piracy. Whatever treasure might have gone down with the Sweet Cutlass is minor when compared with the caches of treasure that ship has sequestered all over the world. All will share in that treasure eventually by the pirate code. In due course, if the Sweet Cutlass miraculously has survived the storm, doubtless, we'll meet her in our adventures because we go after the same prey as she does. Symbolically, the stern piece of the Sweet Cutlass' whaleboat will be enshrined in my cabin."

That was the sum total of the ceremony that I afforded my former vessel. I returned to my duty as Captain of the Night Lightning and ordered full sail with a heading due west to Zanzibar.

I headed to the anchorage just offshore from the port of the old stone city. As soon as I could, I had the coxswain take me ashore so that I could visit Alia and discover the news that had occurred in the time since the Night Lightning had left the port.

When I pulled the bell of her house, Alia came to the door herself and recognized me with a smile. She took me in and seated me at the elevated table above her own little room. She brought me a bottle of rum, and I poured her a glass of rum as I had seen Captain Morgan do when we lasted visited here together.

I told Alia that I feared that Captain Morgan had gone down with his ship and crew during the great storm that had passed through ten days ago. She listened to what I had to say with her usual attention, and after a minute's reflection she raised a toast to Davy Jones. Then she informed me of what had transpired since my last visit.

First, she said that coincidentally the same evening we weighed anchor the port was abuzz with rumors about a mysterious set of killings at the landing. The best part of the crew of a merchantman had been ruthlessly slain, and the killers had escaped in a whaleboat belonging to their ship. Troops had been dispatched too late, and they scoured the waters of the anchorage but found no trace of the killers or the whaleboat. At the time they reached the anchorage, it was too dark to see anything, so the leader of the troops decided to return to the landing and commence a thorough search of the port, the landing and the anchorage the next day at dawn. Alia rolled her eyes as if to suggest that the troops did not have a prayer of finding who did the crimes.

Alia told me that she had been questioned about the killings by a customer from the local garrison. She told him she was nowhere near the landing, so she saw nothing. She said she would report anything that came to her attention or the attention of her women immediately, but nothing had been learned. The Sultan of Zanzibar had been informed of the killings, but his comment was, "The will of Allah be done." After that, the dead men had been buried and the searching by the military was stopped as the troops had other duties and the victims were mere visitors and infidels to boot. The authorities forgot the matter.

The second piece of news had ignited a furious dialog with the foreign powers on the island. Evidently, Alia said, a great many ships that were expected in Africa from the west side of the island did not arrive at their destination. They simply vanished. Certain interests from the African side of the Channel had searched the waters and found no trace of the missing vessels. If only one vessel had disappeared, the Captain and crew of the vessel would have been considered to have turned pirate and stolen the cargo to sell on their own. Under the circumstances of the loss of a dozen vessels, however, some external force was deemed to be operating in the waters, perhaps pirates, but no one could prove this. Alia said that the Sultan of Zanzibar was unimpressed with the rumors that surrounded the disappearance of the ships of his customers. Once business had been conducted, the fate of his customers was in the hands of Allah. The factors on the African side, the great man said, would have to sort out what had happened to their ships because it was none of his affair.

The third piece of news trumped all that Alia said before, and it involved a secret source that the sultan had for slaves. Alia did not know the details, but a particularly strident anti-slavery group was routinely intercepting human traffickers in the Channel and buying the slaves that were destined for Zanzibar. From what Alia gathered, pirates hired by the sultan's operatives had been hired to intercept the English merchant ship that bought the slaves and seize the cargo and slaves to return them to the sultan. When the sultan learned that the pirates had vanished, he became agitated and ordered two of his operatives to be beheaded because he suspected them of paying off the pirates to their own advantage. Since those two operatives were the only persons who knew about the sultan's attempt to seize the slaves from the English, many suspected that they had been killed to cover the sultan's tracks and leave him blameless however things turned out.

Alia said, "I've slept with both of the sultan's operatives, and I learned from them the whole plan, which I thought fantastical at the time. I heard nothing further about the matter, although another customer had told me that the English merchant was back doing business buying slaves and that the sultan was scheming how to stop what they were doing. The sultan is willing to pay a great deal of gold and silver to anyone who will stop the infidel Captain of the English merchantman from doing his dastardly work."

When Alia had let what she had just said sink in and fetched me another bottle of rum, she rubbed her shoeless foot up and down the back of my leg and looked at me in the way women do when they dearly want something from a man. We descended into her little room to sport a while, and when she had done what she wanted to me, I paid her three gold coins, which was what she really wanted, and bid her adieu.

Then I decided to return to my ship to consider the implications of what Alia had told me. I noticed, however, as I left Alia's house that I was being followed to the landing by a shadowy man in a long robe. I pretended to be lost and wandered around the city, but the man kept following me. Finally, I decided to discover what the man wanted, so I ducked into a side street and ran quickly, taking three left turns in succession so that I ended up behind the now-confused man with my knife against his back.

The man decided to communicate with me in half a dozen languages until I recognized the English for, "I am the sultan's man. Touch me and die." Since I had already touched him, I figured that I had nothing to lose now but my life. I asked him why he was following me. He said that he wanted to take me to the sultan through a secret passage into the royal house. So forward we marched, looking like old friends. I kept my knifepoint at his back and held his robe so he could not escape me.

The man was as good as his word. He led me down a path into the city sewer system and proceeded to an entry below ground that had a stairway into a small room on street level. There he told another man in fine silk garments that he had brought the man the sultan wanted to see. I was worried this might be a trap, but I decided to take my chances now and lowered my knife, putting it back in its sheath behind my back.

The man in silk was gone for only a few minutes, and when he returned he gestured that I should come with him, but he held back the shadowy man from proceeding further. I was taken down a narrow corridor to a room that must have been one of the sultan's throne rooms. I was asked to remove my shoes. Soft carpets were piled on the floor except for the polished area around a throne-like chair. In a low commanding voice, the man told me to kneel and bow because the sultan was coming any minute. I bowed and looked up to see the Sultan of Zanzibar himself with a look of amusement on his face.

The man in silk was the interpreter for the brief interchange I had with the sultan. The sultan repeated verbatim the offer that Alia had reported to me—an offer of great riches to rid the sultan of one meddlesome English Captain who was on an infidel crusade to crush the sultan's slave trade, which extended back centuries and gave wealth to everyone who had been involved in it. The sultan said he thought I might be able to do what he wanted done, and he said with amusement that I had a choice. Either I did what he asked and rid him of this infidel and his ship, or I would be taken into the square and beheaded instantly. To make his point, he drew his finger across his neck and smiled, knowing he had been witty.

Through his silky interpreter, I told the sultan that I understood him perfectly, and I knew now of the sultan's infinite wisdom because I was exactly the man he needed to do this job. I asked the sultan two questions in the language I knew he understood above all others: "How much are you willing to pay me right now? And how much will you pay me when the job has been completed?"

The sultan clapped his hands twice, and a woman wearing a veil with most beautiful, oddly familiar black eyes entered with two enormous slaves following. The slaves each carried a chest that, once they were opened, revealed the gold, silver, jewels and pearls that they contained. In one chest was an emerald as big as my fist. In the other chest was a diamond equally large.

The sultan asked me to choose one chest as my retainer, and he said his slave would carry it to my whaleboat for me to take to my ship. He said the other chest would be ready for me to pick up when I brought him proof that I had completed my task. The proof, he said, would be the head of the English Captain of the merchantman that was ruining his slave trade.

I chose the cask with the huge diamond, and the sultan clapped his hands. The slave with the chest with the diamond stood fast while the woman and the other slave with his chest followed the sultan out the door through which they had entered the throne room. Smoothly, the man in silk led me to where my shoes had been deposited, and then he led me out a separate door with the sultan's slave following in my wake. We proceeded unmolested to the place at the landing where my coxswain waited by the whaleboat.

The slave set the chest carefully in the whaleboat and then stood back and waited. After I entered the whaleboat and the coxswain shoved off, the man in silk departed in the direction of the palace with the slave following ten paces behind him. I shuddered when I considered that the slave might have been a mechanical apparatus since he exhibited no sense of himself as a person. For that matter, the man in silk was little different from the slave. Only the veiled woman had shown vitality. Of course, she was Alia, and her vitality might have been due to the exercise we had shared in her little room before she had donned her Arab disguise and returned to the palace.

I realized that I had done what was necessary to escape the sultan's palace alive, but I needed to consider carefully my next moves. Back aboard the Night Lightning in my cabin, I considered my dilemma. I now had a small fortune in the chest that sat on my desk. To the sultan such riches were paltry compared to what he had in store elsewhere. If I were to abscond with the sultan's treasure, I would probably never see him again, and as long as I stayed out of Zanzibar, I would be safe.

If I were to complete the contract I had formed with the sultan, the English Captain would lose his head and I would lose the chance to earn easy money while freeing slaves, but I had no certainty that delivering the man's head would result in the sultan's delivering the second chest to me.

In fact, the more I thought about it, the more I was certain that delivering the infidel's head would seal my fate. I pictured myself being seized by the slave who had carried the chest to my whaleboat and beheaded by the slave's companion because my killing the English Captain was itself a capital offense.

In the end I could see no advantage to the sultan in letting me live another moment after I delivered the promised head. I had witnessed the sultan's mannerisms in Captain Morgan, and I found it somewhat unsettling that the two men acted alike. After all, they were both absolute rulers of their separate domains. Why should they differ as to motives?

The piece of the puzzle that did not fit was Alia. Surely the sultan knew what Alia did in her house of prostitution, and probably he was her sponsor. She was an intelligence asset of the first rate, and her informants knew the intimate thoughts of their customers. Why did the sultan allow Alia to live? Was it her game to be a second Queen Scheherazade? Did she have to struggle to tell the sultan something that he desperately needed to know each time they met to spare herself from a public beheading?

I thought for a few minutes about the advantages of putting the sultan's head in a sack instead of the English

Captain's head, but then I considered the layers of agents and troops that protected the sultan. I stood little chance to survive if I killed the sultan, and what would my killing him gain except freedom from my promise to produce the English Captain's head? The more I thought the matter through, the more flight from Zanzibar seemed the best course of action. In that case, I thought, I should carefully assess what was in the chest to determine what I had gained thus far.

I set the chest on the deck and laid out each item from it on the desk, grouping like with like. My cabin boy watched me with open mouth and bulging eyes as I stacked the gold coins and the silver coins and grouped the diamonds, rubies, sapphires, agates, emeralds and pearls. There was a large bar of solid gold that I let the boy handle so that he would know pure greed and the root of all evil. At the bottom of the chest was a folded piece of paper that contained a note in a familiar hand. I wondered briefly how the note had been slipped into the chest. Was this another trick, or was it a miracle?

The note was written by Captain Morgan in his unmistakable hand. It stated that he was a prisoner in the sultan's dungeon and would be executed if I did not bring the head of the English Captain as the sultan directed. The note went on to say that Alia had betrayed him to the sultan and she would betray anyone to save her own life, which was at hazard every moment. Captain Morgan must have smiled when he wrote the final line, "Of course, the sultan will kill us all when you deliver the English Captain's head, so you figure what must be done."

I knew I had very little time to react to what I had just read, and what I did was automatic because I had no time to think things through.

I told my cabin boy, "Put down the gold bar and fetch the First Mate to my quarters, with the instruction to bring a large burlap sack with him."

When the First Mate came, I showed him the treasure that the sultan had given me. I told him, "I have to accomplish an impossible mission within the next eighteen hours, or everything will be lost. Take command of the Night Lightning and sail this very night out of the anchorage to the sea and return to the anchorage and anchor two hours before dawn. Have the coxswain row me to the landing in the whaleboat and return to the ship. He should stand by to return to the landing so as to be there at first light. There at the landing, I'll meet him when I'm finished with my task."

I had him repeat what I had told him twice. I asked if he had any questions, and he did not.

I told him, "For this service, when I return I'll give you your choice of any one of the items in the chest."

I stowed the valuables in the chest and had the First Mate and one of our freed slaves help me take it to the whaleboat, where the coxswain rowed me and the freed slave to the landing.

In the evening shadows, I watched from the shore as the whaleboat returned to the Night Lightning. I watched the ship unfurl her sails and depart the anchorage. I then ordered the freed slave to carry the chest and follow me. We wound our way through the evening streets to Alia's house. There I pulled the bell. When she answered the door, I put my finger to my lips for silence and whispered that she must hide me, my man and the chest immediately in a place where we could talk.

In a special room that was reserved in Alia's house for secret meetings, I showed Alia the note from Captain Morgan.

I told her, "I want to free him as soon as possible."

"But that is impossible," she said.

I opened the chest with the jewels and watched her eyes widen.

Knowing I had her attention, I pursued my advantage in stern language, "In Zanzibar everything is possible with money, and if you don't help me, I'll kill you right now as the sultan would do if you ever crossed him."

She shuddered and nodded to say she understood me. I told her the outline of my plan, and she agreed to help. What other viable choice did she have?

Right away she dressed in the veiled robe that she wore in the sultan's palace. She led my man and me with the chest through the streets to the secret entrance, through which we reached the palace. She showed me the access way and door to the sultan's chamber and told me that the sultan would be entertaining two of her ladies tonight with no guard on duty because of the impropriety of their activities.

I asked her when the women were scheduled to leave the sultan, and she said they planned to leave at first light as they always did. She said that the man in silk always approached the sultan in this chamber at sunrise to be sure all was well and to brief the sultan on the activities of the day.

When I asked her about the location of Captain Morgan, Alia said the Captain was probably in the underground compartment where special prisoners were kept before they were publicly beheaded. She knew the way there because she had been asked many times to get information from special prisoners before their executions. She said she had not been informed about Captain Morgan's presence in the palace but when she was asked to put his letter into the bottom of the chest by the man in silk, she had read it and discovered the truth. Why the man in silk had included the letter was a mystery to her.

I asked Alia to take my man with the chest to Captain Morgan. She was to pretend the man was her slave, and she was to use whatever she needed from the chest to bribe her way into and out of the prison chamber. I told her to tell the guards that she was on a mission from the sultan himself to question Captain Morgan as she had so many others and that she might need to have her slave bind the man and take him to the sultan if he decided to talk. She liked this plan, and she hurried off with the freed slave while I went directly into the sultan's chamber where he was sporting with the two women in his enormous bed.

I left the three no time to react to my presence. I flew at the sultan and stabbed him in the throat with my drawn knife. Whipping around, I slashed left and right at the necks of the two women. Blood splattered everywhere, but I did not care. As the bodies bled out and the people died grasping at their sliced throats, I backed off the bed and arranged the naked corpses so that the sultan's own knife was now in his hand and each of the women held another of his many knives. The bloody scene appeared as if the three had played rough games and suffered a terrible accident together.

I washed and dried my hands and my knife in the wash room adjoining the bedroom where the bodies lay. I sheathed my knife in the scabbard behind my back and then sat by the door and waited. I admired my handiwork. The sultan deserved to die a worse death. The two women's deaths meant nothing to me. They would have been happy to inform others about what I had done to the sultan. Now they could tell no tales. I also had a plan for their garments.

One hour later Alia arrived with Captain Morgan bound and gagged. My freed slave with the chest came behind them. I covered Alia's mouth so that she could not scream when she saw the tableau that lay on the bed. When Alia had recovered from her initial shock, I took my hand off her mouth and unbound Captain Morgan and removed his gag.

I then told the astonished Captain and my man, "We've no time for explanations. Quickly, pull on the two women's veiled robes."

The four of us proceeded back the way Alia had led me into the palace. We walked through the dark streets as if I were the master of a house, and my three wives followed in my wake at the prescribed distance with the last carrying my chest.

When we arrived at Alia's house, I ordered her to put whatever she wanted to take into a sack and come immediately with us to the landing. There at first light as we had planned, the First Mate stepped ashore from the whaleboat, and we all climbed in to row to the Night Lightning.

We had just climbed aboard the ship when the cannons at the fort fired shots of alarm. The port and landing area soon became a frenzy of activity. Shouting filled the city behind the port.

Calmly, I ordered the First Mate to weigh anchor and clear the anchorage as rapidly as possible. Since the sails were still unfurled, the ship was tugging seaward in the morning breeze. When the anchor broke free the ship rocked forward, gaining momentum.

I took Captain Morgan and Alia to my cabin with my man following with the chest. There I opened the chest and gave my man his choice of any of the items inside it. He chose the largest of the pearls and put it in a pouch that hung from his side. I told him to return to his duty station, and he smiled broadly and left.

When the First Mate came to report that the ship was underway and out of the anchorage heading for open water, I asked him to select one item from the chest. He chose a large ruby. My cabin boy watched all this with open mouth. He had never heard of such largesse even in the most outlandish fairy tales.

Now I turned to Alia and Captain Morgan and shrugged. "We have a lot of catching up to do. Are you as thirsty as I am?"

"We're parched!"

So I told the cabin boy, "Fetch three bottles of rum and a loaf of bread."

The ship was out in the ocean now, so I excused myself to visit the helm and order the mate of the watch to follow the shore to the south to the southernmost point of the island and then turn north and follow along the shore in the Zanzibar Channel. When that was clear, I returned to my cabin to find the Captain and Alia drinking rum and talking about the woman's future.

"Captain, I want to know what had happened to the Sweet Cutlass."

"First, let me raise a toast to the man in silk. Now there was a man who knew how to take revenge like a pirate." He raised his bottle and drank deeply from it.

I suddenly saw the light, and I eagerly drank to the man's health as well.

The sun was now rising fully above the horizon, and behind us the cannons were booming in frustration because the sultan had been found dead in his bed. We were not frustrated because we had together done the impossible and freed a grateful man and a grateful woman, and all it had cost was one bar of gold and one fist-sized diamond as bribes from a chest that still brimmed with valuables. It was now time to eat, drink, be merry and tell a few tales.

The cabin boy was chewing on a crust of bread in anxious anticipation of hearing lore. Alia ruffled the boy's hair and smiled. She who had survived by telling tales now was as eager as the boy to hear others tell a few. So now it was Captain Morgan's time to tell tales.

He told us about how the Sweet Cutlass had ridden out the terrible storm and how, like the Night Lightning, he had plotted a course to the Arabian Gulf. His was a story with a hundred other stories packed inside it.

Like me, he had decided to deal with the sultan directly. He had left his First Mate in charge of his ship with orders to sail to Zanzibar Island. He had been betrayed by the same man who led me to the sultan. He had seen at close quarters the debauchery of the sultan's court.

The sultan had ordered him to be beheaded, and the only way he could survive was to tell tales of the sea each night in the manner of the woman storyteller in the Thousand and One Nights. The greatest indignity was the lack of rum at the palace. The sultan, though abstinent in liquor, was a debaucher of the first class, only his preference was for men, not women. That led to the Captain's having to fend his host off by singing pirate songs. Fortunately, he was able to write the note that Abe had found. That made the miracle of his escape possible.

So all the way around Zanzibar Island to where the Sweet Cutlass lay at anchor on the west side of the Zanzibar Channel, he regaled us nonstop.

He was still talking when we anchored next to our sister ship, and when he descended into the whaleboat with Alia, the chest and the stern piece from his former whaleboat with the name of his ship carved in it. The coxswain rowed him back to his ship while I watched by the helm.

The coxswain told me when he returned to the Night Lightning that Captain Morgan was talking even when he and Alia were hauled onto the deck of the Sweet Cutlass. For all his garrulity, the wily old Captain never fully answered the question I had asked him.

After what I had been through, I decided I did not really care. I knew what I had done, and all I really needed to know was that we were back in the pirate business now. It felt really good to get my sea legs back on the deck of my own ship.

Chapter Six
Pirates of Arabia

/ know of no waters like those of the vast Persian Gulf. Aquatic life is so abundant from the surface in almost indistinguishable layers right to the depths, where fish play among colorful coral formations visible from the surface.

The ships Night Lightning and Sweet Cutlass had taken prizes in those waters and in the Arabian Sea that lay to the south of them for just over one month. We focused first on the outbound traffic from the Sultanate of Oman, but gradually our emphasis shifted to preying upon the much more lucrative trade of the pirates along the southern gulf coast.

Those pirates ran gold from a certain sheikdom to India, which could never seem to get enough of the yellow metal. In this congenial gulf sheikdom a finite amount of gold and silver bought refuge and, more importantly, loose women and liquor. We pirates could and did for a while gain intelligence and feast upon the international shipping vessels from all over the world. We also had rum and women whenever we liked and a steady stream of actionable intelligence from an unlikely source.

I found living among believers in Islam pleasant only when we had an understanding with the local authorities that allowed us to do whatever we wanted.

For sufficient treasure in our sheikdom we became immune to religious strictures because our sponsors and protectors sheltered us from them. While they beat, maimed or killed their own believers for minor infractions, they left us alone for gold. In the right sheikdom with the right arrangement, we could also repair our ships and get some needed rest and relaxation between our marauding efforts in the gulf and the sea that otherwise would have been impossible for pirates without patronage.

When we arrived, we had no contacts that mattered in the Persian Gulf, and we had arrived here by traveling the long way around from Zanzibar Island. We followed the heavily trafficked sea-lanes through the Indian Ocean, taking our prizes all the way from Zanzibar to Oman.

We then checked out that Omani sultanate, since it was closely connected to the slave trade of Zanzibar as well as all of Arabia. We saw many wondrous things in our voyage, such as sea serpents grey in color as smooth as polished brass and as long as our ship the Night Lightning, the cold fire that lit up all the masts like lightning at night or the phosphor.

Of these three phenomena the phosphor was the most mysterious and fatal to my hearties. Our entire time in the magical realm of Arabia was like the night the phosphor came, and I should have taken it as the warning that it was, but I was naïve and blind to the consequences of its secret message.

According to the Night Lightning's log, my ship entered the cloud of phosphorescence around midnight on the 31st of October in the Arabian Sea well south of Oman. The white, fog-like substance permeated the exterior and interior spaces of the Night Lightning, and you could feel a tension all over the ship. No one dared make a sound, and any normal sound was muffled by the surrounding, glowing whiteness.

Captain Morgan had told me over a bottle of rum that he had encountered the phenomenon before in the Persian Gulf and also in the Arabian Sea. That night from my preferred place near the helm, I sent a message around to all my crew that the phosphorescence was normal in these waters and that everything was going to be all right. In retrospect that was a false message that may have cost my hearties their lives.

When one giant, white tentacle reached out and grasped my port lookout, a few seconds elapsed before I could register what was happening. My starboard lookout was taken next. His scream was quickly muffled as he went below the water's surface. Huge, long tentacles now blindly groped everywhere from focsle to fantail and from the weather decks to the crow's nest.

My helmsman was snatched away screaming by one white tentacle. I saw another white tentacle exploring the area around the helm. I dodged the slimy, white, living thing, glad that it had no eyes. It slapped the deck looking for prey. It tried but failed to grasp me at the helm where I stood fast, frozen with fear at its ghostly presence. It was like the hand of a wicked drunken man whose intent was to kill whatever it found. But it passed, and I felt the relief of one who has been reprieved.

Then for a while all was quiet in the cottony cloud. Below on the weather decks I heard the tentacles' characteristic thump-thump-thumping. If the tentacles had reached the below-decks spaces, I thought, it would by now have reached the crew's quarters also. My entire crew might have been taken by a white phosphorescent sea monster. I stood by the helm like a bird fascinated by a viper. I could do nothing to stop what was happening. I could only wait out the night and hope for the best.

Meanwhile the Night Lightning made no headway in the white shroud because there were no winds and no currents.

When the sun burned through the white the next morning, my hearties, still in shock from the events of the previous night, came from below decks and found me all alone above decks at the helm. Like all sailors everywhere, they were superstitious about the signs of bad events to come. The phosphor had disappeared, taking seven of my hearties with it to see Davy Jones. I ordered the crew to look lively and man their normal watch stations. It had been a very close thing to have survived the night. I did not want to experience the phosphor ever again.

The phosphor was not the only lethal phenomenon we met on this voyage. Within the Persian Gulf another day the tiny, poisonous sea snakes bred. You could see them spread upon the surface and through the upper layer of the hot, salt water like an iridescent, wriggling skein.

Local people warned us not to swim when the water snakes hatched because they could bite a bare ear or toe and inject poisonous venom that would kill. Like everything else in the teeming vat of life that was the Persian Gulf, fish ate those snakes and then were eaten by other, larger fish.

More dangerous to my ship though than the poisonous water snakes was the daytime fog that seemed to boil up from the gulf on days so hot I thought the entire waterway would evaporate into salt. Pursuing merchant vessels into that fog was a losing game if the merchant's Captain knew his soundings and sped his ship towards shore. Yet in just such a fog my socked-in ship happened across a curious dhow manned by local pirates.

We took that dhow as our prize and found aboard it below decks gold in every conceivable form—bars, coins, dust and ore. The dhow's Captain and crew pled that they were under the sheik's protection, but that merely sealed their fate in our minds. We could not become known as pirates who raided the sheik's own ships. After we shipped the dhow's gold aboard the Night Lightning, we forced those pirates to walk the plank and scuttled their craft to eliminate all evidence of our piracy. When the fog broke that evening and the stars appeared in the clear, black Arabian skies, no evidence remained of our piracy, and we believed we had struck a gold seam that demanded our immediate and strict attention.

The sheik that we had bought dearly harbored a house of pleasure worked by beautiful foreign women who serviced all the sailors who visited the sheikdom. They gave pleasure for gold and silver coins of all nations and precious jewels or pearls as well. All of the women workers were infidels from Europe, Asia and America. They did not care whether their customers were Muslims, Christians or Jews; they only cared about the color of their customers' money. These women knew many languages and listened closely when their customers spoke. They collected intelligence nightly.

Alia understood them because she belonged as one of their sisterhood except that, unlike them, she was born a Muslim.

Since Captain Morgan and I had rescued this Scheherazade from what was essentially slavery to the now-deceased Sultan of Zanzibar, she had lived aboard the Sweet Cutlass in Captain Morgan's cabin and was considered one of our pirate crew with an equal share of the booty that we stole. She earned her share doing what no hearty could have done.

In the gulf when we anchored, out Alia went ashore dressed in her veiled robe. She befriended the women in the house of pleasure, sponsored and protected by the sheik, to discover valuable intelligence that we pirates could put to good use.

When Captain Morgan visited the house, he remained in the great room near the entrance entertaining the guests while his veiled, supposed wife Alia slipped into the back rooms, where the women waited and rested between entertaining their customers to garner whatever intelligence would help us in our trade.

In this way she learned about the dhows from the sheikdom that plied the gold trade into India. She was told the location of the storehouse where the gold was readied for shipment. She learned how the gold was transported to that storehouse in the sheikdom by water and by land. Because one of the woman of the house or pleasure was favored by the sheik himself, she had learned firsthand how the sheik profited from his smuggling operations. Alia learned from her that the sheik was frenetically concerned that a special shipment of gold had vanished without leaving a trace.

The sheik was a bearded man small in stature but with an enormous capacity for rage. When he learned that his special gold shipment had never reached India, he identified ten men who he thought might have conspired to steal the gold and beheaded them all with his own curved sword.

That was the same special gold shipment that had been seized by my hearties, but we had been very careful to destroy all evidence of our crime. We had also taken pains not to exhibit any of the loot we had plundered from the dhow in the sheikdom or anywhere else in the Persian Gulf region, because doing so might have been fatal to our business and our lives.

Yet Alia's new female contacts gave her details about the timing of the sheik's gold shipments that turned out to be accurate, so we made it our business routinely to harvest the sheik's gold.

We did not capture every dhow. In fact, we let every other shipment pass through our two-ship moving cordon into India to keep the sheik in business. As long as the sheik continued to send out his dhows, we amassed wealth from our piracy. So we had to keep tabs on the sheik's thoughts and strategies. The sheik was vigilant and vengeful as well as greedy and devious. He was inordinately attentive toward his gold.

On one visit to the house of pleasure, while Captain Morgan drank rum, smoked, told tall tales and swore in the drawing room to an appreciative audience, Alia was asked by the female consort of the sheik whether she knew of anyone who could provide security for the sheik's gold shipments.

Alia told the woman that she would check around. Perhaps, Alia said enigmatically, something could be done for the right price.

Late that night when Captain Morgan and Alia were rowed out to the Sweet Cutlass in the whaleboat by my coxswain, Alia outlined the plan that the sheik's woman had suggested to her.

In turn the coxswain told me what he had overheard. In essence the sheik was so desperate for help that he was willing to give up one quarter of his gold from his gold trade to protect it. His rationale was that he was already losing half his gold and that he would gain back that half for the contribution of a quarter for guaranteed protection. He figured that would leave him a quarter ahead of the current state of the game.

On their next visit to the house of pleasure, Alia told the consort of the sheik that Captain Morgan would be just the man to provide security for the gold trade. His proposed terms to the sheik were to receive one quarter of each gold shipment in advance as a fee for assuring that it reached India as planned.

The sheik asked to meet Captain Morgan, and they rode camels together deep into the desert to the oasis called Al Ain. The men got to know each other, and the sheik liked the Captain for his candor and confidence. So the two men bargained and struck a deal for protection of the sheik's gold traffic, with one important change from Captain Morgan's original proposal. Instead of receiving the full quarter before a shipment departed, Captain Morgan would receive one eighth. A second eighth would be due upon delivery of the gold in India. If a shipment for any reason did not arrive, then Captain Morgan would forfeit the eighth he had collected in advance. After the shipment had been delivered, Captain Morgan's interest in the business ended. Once their agreement had been sealed, the sheik and the Captain rode out of the desert on their camels, and the Captain returned to his ship to execute on their plan.

For a while their plan worked perfectly. Captain Morgan collected half his fee, and he escorted the dhow carrying the gold shipment to India, where he collected the rest of his fee. On its return voyage the Sweet Cutlass would prowl and take prizes of opportunity. Meanwhile the Night Lightning would shadow the protection operation, taking prizes as it could but basically assuring that no other pirates would attack either the Sweet Cutlass or the dhow with its cargo of gold. Not long after we had begun our program, it occurred to me that the most valuable target on our home voyages was the same dhow that took the gold to India because it returned with greater than equal value of the outgoing gold in its hold. So every other trip the Night Lightning would harvest the contents of the returning dhow, kill its crew and scuttle the vessel.

After the third such seizure and destruction effort against returning dhows, Captain Morgan and Alia visited the sheik's house of pleasure where they learned from the sheik's female consort that the sheik was beside himself with rage about the loss of the cargo on his returning dhows. The sheik, she said, was satisfied that he had bought the security of his outgoing dhows, but he now wanted to buy the security of his incoming dhows as well.

Alia told the woman that the sheik could probably negotiate the same deal for the returning dhows as he had for the outgoing dhows with Captain Morgan. The sheik demanded another meeting with the Captain at the oasis, and there he bargained for the same deal, aware that once he cut this deal he would be no better off than he was when he cut the first deal, since he would effectively have paid half of his trade in protection money. Nevertheless, the deal was struck, and the two men returned from the desert satisfied with their bargain.

For four months the sheik's gold trafficking business went swimmingly. I was mildly annoyed to see that we were taking only half of the treasure that was flowing between the sheik and his Indian factors. I wondered how we might increase our rewards by taking a bolder, more inventive strategy than this relatively safe harvesting strategy. I began scheming about how to increase our share without driving the sheik insane.

If he reneged on our current deals, we would be a lot worse off than we were before we started the enforcement actions that protected his gold shipments.

So I anchored the Night Lightning off the Indian port where the dhows unloaded their cargoes, and I went ashore alone to investigate what happened to the gold after it had been offloaded from the dhows and delivered to the Indian factors that paid for the cargo. I pretended to be a merchant looking to barter my wares, and I took along samples including gold.

Of course, the Indian merchants only wanted to deal with me for the gold because they had other sources for all other commodities I had to offer them. They were eager to drive a bargain, but I held out for a fraction more than I knew the sheik was receiving for his gold.

We agreed to terms, so I went back to the Night Lightning and fetched a whaleboat full of gold in all forms. The cargo was handled and guarded by two of my hearties, who were among our former slaves.

The transaction went as I had planned, and I sent one of my hearties to witness where the gold had been taken after I had sold it. He returned to report that the gold was escorted to an imposing edifice with gables near the port gateway. I conjectured that a small raiding party might liberate the gold we had just sold and other gold and valuables in the imposing edifice as well, but I prudently wanted to know more about the disposition of the gold before I acted.

I therefore went back out to the ship in the whaleboat with the large bags of jewels and pearls that had bought the gold, and at midnight I returned to the port to check out the imposing edifice where my gold had been taken.

I saw that the gold was being transported that very night in a kind of caravan. The heavy metal was loaded onto carts and onto the backs of animals and bearers in heavy sacks and boxes. Armed men guarded the house, the road and the caravan itself. If I had brought my small force, we would not have stood a chance to overcome the security and seize the gold.

Clearly, I thought, the gold was controlled by very powerful people who knew the value of their enterprise and paid well to enforce it. I decided to follow the caravan to see where it was going with the gold. Perhaps, I thought at the time, the gold was heading for a place where other gold had been deposited. Raiding that place might be less risky than raiding the imposing edifice, I thought.

The gold was taken through the night to a huge marketplace where many kinds of goods were set out for sale. I saw that the gold was sold from an enclosure that was very secure and well-guarded.

During the morning, merchants went into the enclosure and came out with small lots of the gold. I deduced that liberating the gold in the enclosure would be too risky for my hearties and that stealing from the many buyers would provide too paltry award for the many efforts it would take. Ships can carry much larger volumes of gold and anything else than other mode of transport, and we pirates know how to capture and pillage a ship.

I had to admit that there was no percentage for my crew working to liberate the gold ashore in India, so I returned to the port and roused my sleeping coxswain to row me back out to my ship. There I brooded all day while I watched other ships arrive and depart.

It was late afternoon that I espied through my spyglass an interesting exchange of very heavy parcels that had been transferred from an anchored ship. Unless the ship was dealing in ingots of lead, I thought, the ship's cargo was surely gold. I surveyed the ship where the cargo originated, and I decided that the Night Lightning would make it a prize to determine its business. The ship flew a Spanish flag, but that did not mean much to me because I routinely used false flags to avoid being remarked as a pirate—until it was time to raise the Jolly Roger in the prospect of a raid.

So when the Spanish-flagged ship I had targeted weighed anchor, my hearties heaved ho as well, and we sailed off in pursuit. When we were out of sight of land, the ship rigged to full sail and closed with the ship as we prepared to board her. My hearties rushed to their battle stations and raised the Jolly Roger. We overtook the vessel and grappled our way close alongside it, with my hearties swinging aboard with cutlasses and knives drawn.

Subduing the Captain and crew was easy, and my hearties knew the drill for dealing with a prize ship. Within an hour, the Captain and the crew of the prize had been sent to see Davy Jones, and all treasure and valuables from the prize had been transferred to the Night Lightning. As a special trophy, the First Mate brought me the Captain's log from the prize ship's Captain's cabin.

From the log entries, it was clear that the ship had made regular monthly scheduled passages between Oman and India. Specifically, it had carried gold to the east and jewels and pearls to the west. It had also on one prior trip carried a baby elephant from India to Oman.

My crew discovered only token amounts of gold aboard the prize because all its gold had been transferred to factors at the Indian port. I deduced from this that I should plan to raid the replacement for this vessel during the next scheduled passage from Oman, which was scheduled to occur one month hence.

Back in the sheikdom, I learned that Captain Morgan was becoming bored with the new routine of protecting the sheik's gold traffic. At the house of pleasure after having consumed two bottles of rum, the Captain began railing about the pedestrian nature of a life without danger and daring. He decided it was time to fire his pistol in the house and stand on a table brandishing his cutlass and singing boisterous, lewd pirate songs. With his parrot perched on his shoulder, Benjamin laughed and pointed at his Captain on the table, egging him on.

Things might have gotten out of hand, but I calmed down both the Captain and his man, and I whispered to Captain Morgan that I had another game than security in mind that might please him well enough. I then told him about the Spanish-flagged vessel I had captured and sunk and about the log entries indicating the monthly passage of gold passing from Oman to India. The Captain scowled and ran his hand over his beard.

When the light of realization came into his eyes, he ordered two more bottles of rum, one for me and one for himself. We drank the rum and plotted head to head until it was time for us to leave the house and return to our ships.

Alia had also learned a few things that would come in handy, so all-in-all it was a good night's work, though Captain Morgan with his antics had risked the ruin of our whole livelihood with a few choice words in the wrong public environment.

I feared that the sheik's female consort, who had overheard the Captain's remarks about piracy, might be smart enough to understand our subterfuge and greedy enough to inform the sheik about our piratical escapades.

We planned carefully for our raid on the next scheduled Omani gold run. The complication was that the sheik's dhow was going to be in transit during the same interval as the gold shipment from Oman. That meant that we had to navigate so as to protect the sheik's dhow while capturing our prize.

As often happens when the perfect plan hits the reality of operations, we met with surprises and had to improvise.

Specifically, another pirate decided it was time to move against our sheik's dhow, and the Omani ship was found sailing in tandem with a ship from Muscat.

My lookout spied the three ships coming from different directions across our track. The Night Lightning would ordinarily have interdicted the pirate ship, but I figured that the Sweet Cutlass would be able to handle our security job. I therefore hoisted the Jolly Roger and steered to intercept the ships from Oman and Muscat, both of which were armed with cannon.

The winds were in my favor, and with full sail the Night Lightning cut right across the bow of the ship from Muscat, firing a salvo that took out the main brace and caused significant crew loss at the same time.

With that ship unable to maneuver, the Night Lightning continued at speed to ram and board the ship from Oman, which chose to fire cannon balls rather than scrap metal, nails and chains as we did. The result was futile whistling as the cannon balls passed over our lower decks without causing damage.

My hearties used grappling hooks and lines to swing from ship to ship, and the boarding party led by the First Mate began to savage the crew with their cutlasses and knives. I had the remainder of my hearties cut free from the Omani ship, and I tacked to intercept and board the ship from Muscat.

My Second Mate led the second boarding party, and they arrived on board their prize with such ferocity that the remaining crew threw down their weapons and begged for mercy. Mercifully, then, my hearties cut them down to the last man and threw their bodies overboard. They raced to search the ship for gold and other valuables.

In the distance I heard a cannon's report and saw my First Mate signal. The First Mate was ready to transfer the Omani ship's cargo when I was ready to receive it. His small prize crew had clearly managed to take control of the ship's navigation and cannon, but the ship was now sailing in a direction away from our position rather than towards it. I urged the Second Mate and his hearties to hurry while I swept the horizon with my spyglass.

From the crow's nest I heard, "Ship ahoy two points off the starboard bow!"

I swung my spyglass to see that a warship was approaching the Omani vessel with full sail. I called to my Second Mate that I would be back.

My remaining hearties cut free from the ship from Muscat, and we proceeded with full sail to intercept the warship before it caught up with the Omani ship.

"Gunners, fire one free shot to get the warship's attention." I hoped to divert that ship from pursuing the Omani ship and make it turn and fight us at a disadvantage because of the wind. My ploy worked, and I saw the warship come about.

It fired a broadside as its guns to port became unmasked, but its sails slacked for lack of wind. As its gunners reloaded, we gained enough advantage to get a shot off from our port cannon as I came right. The shot hit home on the vessel's main brace and brought the warship dead in the water, and that was my intent.

As I passed astern of the crippled vessel, I tacked to bring my stern around to face her. I ordered sails rigged to proceed as best possible, keeping our stern pointed at the warship's stern. Through my spyglass I saw the warship's crew trying vainly to splice the main brace, and I knew that once out of the range of the warship's cannons, I could proceed as I wished.

The helm steered for the Omani ship and kept a constant bearing to close while we plied full sail to meet her. Seeing the Night Lightning approach, my First Mate brought the Omani ship around so he and the prize crew could do their transfer and board us. For a moment I did not see the prize crew on the weather decks, and I surmised that they were below decks scuttling the Omani vessel. When they appeared again, the First Mate and his prize crew made great haste to do the transfer of the gold and scamper back aboard.

After we cut away from her, the Omani ship began to list as it took on water, and soon it lay for a time at an acute angle as it sank beneath the waves to descend slowly to meet Davy Jones. By then I had turned the Night Lightning to give a wide berth to the crippled warship.

When I had passed the closest point of approach to the warship, I turned the ship and began maneuvering her to the area where I had left the ship from Muscat in the capable hands of my Second Mate and his prize crew.

That ship was not visible on the horizon, so I called to the lookout in the crow's nest to keep his eyes peeled to all points off the bow as we pressed forward, tacking back and forth against the prevailing contrary wind.

Finally, the lookout called out, "Boat ahoy off the bow!"

I could not make out a contact through my spyglass, so I called for the lookout to point at the boat and keep pointing while I tacked to close the distance.

Tacking frequently was rough going, but finally I made out a whaleboat coming towards us with a man waving in it. The man was my Second Mate. His prize crew and cargo were weighing the boat perilously deep in the water. When it was clear that the ship was going to close successfully with the boat, the Second Mate and his hearties jumped out of the whaleboat and held onto its sides to give her more freeboard and keep her from being overwhelmed and sunk by the wave action of the ocean.

In these shark-infested waters, dangling like bait from the side of a boat was a courageous maneuver to save a large cargo of gold from going to the bottom. I urged the men to work fast hauling both the hearties and the gold aboard. We paid out a hawser to tow the whaleboat behind the Night Lightning, which was quickly gaining speed to intercept the Sweet Cutlass somewhere over the eastern horizon between here and the port of India.

The first indication that we were on the right track was the flotsam from the pirate ship that had tried to intercept the sheik's dhow. Captain Morgan had clearly made quick work of that ship of fools and sent them to Davy Jones. The question was, were the Sweet Cutlass and the dhow safe?

It was late afternoon as I approached the anchorage outside the Indian port that I got the answer to my question. There where it had last set its anchor lay the Sweet Cutlass with her Captain and crew arrayed on deck, eating and drinking as if they were on a pleasure cruise. After I set anchor not far from my sister ship, secured the sailing watch and set the anchor watch, Captain Morgan set out in his whaleboat to see what plunder I had taken. Alia in her veiled robe and Benjamin with his parrot came along for the ride.

As evening came, we all sat in my cabin with my cabin boy. My First Mate came to the cabin to present the best of his pelf first—eight large sacks of gold coins and three of gold dust from the hold of the Omani ship. He described many other valuables he had taken, and to prove the worth of his discoveries, he showed an enormous ruby, which he placed on my chart table next to my log. I rewarded him with permission to broach a cask of rum with his prize crew for their efforts, and he went off quickly to begin the celebration.

Then my Second Mate came to the cabin to present the best of his pelf—a dozen strong boxes containing golden bars and a sack full of almost perfect pearls, one of which was as large as a cherry. Captain Morgan looked on with approval at the pelf, but he asked with an accusatory look what had happened to the ship from Muscat. The Second Mate said resignedly that when his prize crew went below to scuttle the ship, they found that the Muscat crew had already done that work and the ship was sinking fast. It was all he and his hearties could do to transfer the cargo to the whaleboat and escape the sinking vessel before it disappeared beneath the waves.

I told Captain Morgan about the man's having jumped into the water with his hearties to keep enough freeboard so that the whaleboat did not sink. At this Captain Morgan frowned and said they were lucky not to have been devoured by sharks. The Second Mate smiled and said they were luckier still to have been found by his Captain. They had run out of rum by the time he found them. At this hint, I rewarded the Second Mate and his prize crew with permission to broach a cask of rum. That pleased the man greatly, and he hastened to begin the night's drinking with his hearties.

The Third Mate came next to describe what we had all done aboard the Night Lightning while the First Mate and Second Mate and their prize crews were busy killing men and taking plunder. Captain Morgan was very impressed to discover my tactics when the warship appeared. He said a few words about it being a pity to leave the ship above the waves when it deserved richly to go beneath them.

I laughed and told the Captain that it was better to have treasure than revenge. He retorted that it was best to have both treasure and revenge.

Then Benjamin's parrot said distinctly, "Bottle of rum!" We all drank to that, and I sent my cabin boy below to fetch a feast, which we shared while we listened to Captain Morgan's tale of boarding the pirate vessel, killing her Captain and all of her crew and taking aboard her treasure hoard. To give panache and point to his story, he asked Alia to show everyone what was in the leather pouch she carried around her neck. She opened her pouch with great drama, pulled it open and shook out five enormous diamonds and a great emerald into her hand. The Captain then asked Benjamin to tell everyone what else that ship contained.

Benjamin rose to the occasion with his bird on his shoulder and smiled. He said the enemy pirate ship had contained many barrels, kegs and bottles of rum, five tuns full of malmsey, dried and salted fish, dates and apricots, bags of sundry grains and an armory of guns, powder, swords and very sharp knives. Benjamin smiled when he described the rich garments, animal hides and materials, colorful African bird feathers, six caged love birds, three pet green monkeys, four chimpanzees and a pair of gorillas.

His face clouded over when he said, "We also found deep in the hold six slaves, four males and two females. They were bound together in tight-fitting chains."

Seeing that Benjamin was now feeling profound emotions, Captain Morgan said, "Those men and women are now free of their chains and resting on the weather decks of the Sweet Cutlass. They've been given food and water and rum. Alia has provided the women with robes, and the crew donated their old clothes for the men to wear."

Without looking at Benjamin, the Captain said with a fierce look that brooked no opposition, "Those fine men and women will never be slaves again." The Captain went on to say, "I received our recompense for safe delivery of the dhow's gold to the Indian factors and for escorting the dhow on its return voyage. Since the dhow is not scheduled to return to the sheikdom until three days hence, I want Abe to show me the local sights with particular attention to the port's gold repository." That was the imposing edifice I had described to him.

So early the next morning Captain Morgan and I went ashore to survey the imposing edifice. We walked all around the edifice discussing the merits of piracy over robbery, but I saw a familiar glitter in the Captain's eyes when I told him how much gold I had seen taken from this building and conveyed by that caravan to the great open-air market that lay a night's march away. I reviewed the security features of the edifice and the procedures that accompanied the transfer of the gold from port to edifice, from edifice to caravan and from caravan to market compound.

The Captain observed, "Among the clothing we seized from the pirate ship are garments worn by Islamic merchants. Where might we find two dromedary camels?" I knew what he was thinking. Once the Captain made up his mind, there was no changing it, but I reflected what the short remainder of our lives would be like in a filthy Indian jail while we awaited execution for murder and theft. That being said, I had no doubts or misgivings about the Captain's plans. His mind was still sharp and running far ahead of all others.

Since our First Mates had been left in charge of our ships, we had no compunction about staying ashore overnight. Just as before, I watched the nighttime transfer of the gold from the edifice to the caravan, only this time Captain Morgan's eyes watched the process with mine. He pointed out where the vulnerabilities in the process lay. Then we shadowed the slow procession of the caravan to the marketplace, and Captain Morgan again remarked on the vulnerabilities in the bends of the path and the darkness between the torches that the security guards carried. Around one o'clock in the morning a group of a dozen brigands attacked the caravan, and they were easily killed or repulsed by the guards.

The Captain shook his head at the clumsiness of the brigands' approach. "They're not really professionals, but a ragtag group probably trying robbery for the first and last time. We should break off from following the caravan and instead follow the two brigands who escaped being killed."

One of the surviving brigands had been wounded. He was bleeding badly and growing weaker with every step. His companion saw that the man would die, so he drew his knife and slit the man's throat. He left the man's body in the vegetation by the side of the trail and went forward with us following him right to his hideout in the forest.

He was met there by three men and two women with torches. They seemed to berate him for having been unsuccessful in his venture. All went into a makeshift building where they evidently lived and stored their ill-gotten wealth.

Captain Morgan drew his knife and went for a visit. I followed him through the door with my own knife drawn. Inside the building we surprised the six people and had no trouble killing them all. They were not hardened by fighting at close quarters as pirates are inured to doing.

We quickly surveyed the stores their group had amassed, and we were pleasantly surprised to find among them gold and silver that they had presumably stolen from other caravans. The brigands were surely not amateurs as we had thought.

In fact, there were so many sacks of riches there that we could not carry away more than a fraction at a time. So we found a place under the roots of a huge tree where we could hide what we had found, and we made two score trips from the building to the tree carrying heavy sacks and parcels. Finally, we selected four huge bags of gold coins to take with us on our return to the port.

By morning we reached our whaleboat, where we roused our coxswain to row us to our ships with the gold. We did not wait on our ships but brought a prize crew of twelve in two whaleboats, one of which was from the ship from Muscat. We went back to the brigand's hideout, where we discovered that other brigands had come looking for their brethren. We were glad that we had found a hiding place for the gold that was not visible from the main building.

Stealthily we went to our hoard under the tree roots and, each man taking two huge bags of gold, we retraced our steps and returned to our whaleboats. By the time we reached our ships, it was evening, but a pirate's work is never done.

So once again Captain Morgan and I returned to the shore and went back into the forest to the brigands' building. The brigands were absent when we arrived at their hide, so we waited outside and watched for their return. In the very early morning, but well before dawn, a dozen of the brigands did return, carrying heavy bags and two badly wounded men. While the men carried their bags into the building, the man we thought was their leader dispatched the two wounded men by slitting their throats. He ordered the others to bury the two bodies in the forest. As his men scurried off, he sauntered into the building.

"Captain, I think eight men are occupied burying the bodies. Four men including the leader are now inside the building with the treasure."

I could not make out the Captain's face in the darkness, but I heard his familiar, "Yaar!" I felt him move forward and I knew his knife was drawn, but I managed to pull him down just as another group of brigands came out of the forest from behind the building with more treasure.

I could not believe our good luck. We had narrowly missed being detected, and the treasure we had come for was increasing by the hour. We lay flat, watching as the leader of the second group of brigands and the leader of the first group emerged from the building to talk strategy in a language neither of us understood.

The upshot of their discussions was evidently that they would take their groups back immediately to make another raid on the caravan before first light. I thought that was a very bad plan from a pirate's point of view because of the visibility that daybreak gave to the defenders.

We, on the other hand, were fortunate because the brigands were going to leave their store unguarded, and we had the rest of the night to remove the treasure from the house to our secret hiding place under the roots of the giant tree.

When the men who had been sent to bury their dead comrades returned, they joined the brigands who were waiting to get back to raiding. The two groups departed as a single force in the direction of the main path through the forest.

We waited to be sure none would circle back to their building, but none did return. We then went up to the door of the building, but Captain Morgan cautioned me about barging right in. Instead, he looked for another entrance. There was a high window with a sill.

The Captain forced the wooden covering over the window, and together we entered through the orifice that was revealed behind it. The Captain struck flint on steel and started a flame, with which he lit a candle that he had brought for the purpose. He showed me with his light how the brigands had rigged a devilish booby trap inside the front entrance that would impale anyone who opened the door. I shuddered to think what would have happened if the Captain had not stopped me. He disarmed the device temporarily so that we could use the door to remove the gold, and then he produced a large, red candle by which we would be working to remove the gold.

We hurried to carry the heavy bags of treasure through the door to hide them in the place beneath the tree roots. We worked hard for over two hours to clear all the treasure out of the building. Aside from the pelf we stored under the tree roots, we left four sacks of gold bars on the ground in front of the building. Satisfied that we had not missed anything, the Captain carefully closed the front door and rearmed the devilish booby trap in such a way that anyone trying to disarm it from the outside would trigger the device.

Leaving our large, red candle burning on the floor as a kind of token, we climbed out of the building through the window that had let us inside, and the Captain and I restored the wood covering over the orifice. We took the four huge sacks of gold bars that we had laid aside with us as we departed the area.

We saw no sign of the brigands as we returned all the way back to the landing, where our coxswain was waiting for us. He rowed us to the Sweet Cutlass, where we decided that we would return that very night with enough hearties to carry all the gold we had hidden back to the whaleboats, of which we would need three this time instead of two.

I was once again glad that I had towed the whaleboat from the Muscat to the anchorage behind the Night Lightning. The Captain summoned Benjamin to muster a party of twenty strong men to do the heavy lifting and asked me to return to my ship and bring ten men in my own whaleboat for the venture. With ten men in each of three whaleboats, we shoved off an hour before nightfall and landed on shore, where we set out in three parties so as not to arouse suspicions about our intentions. We formed a single group on the main path around an hour's walk from the port, and the Captain led us to the area where the brigands' building lay.

While the hearties hid and waited, the Captain and I went forward to get a view of the building. There, as we saw from hiding, the two groups of brigands, approximately forty of them, sat in circular rows around a large bonfire they had built in the clearing in front of the building. We could make out two men sitting on the ground outside the circular groups that surrounded the fire.

I recognized the bound men as the leaders of the two groups. The brigands had evidently decided that their leaders had betrayed them by spiriting away their gold.

While we watched, four brigands lifted each man and threw him into the bonfire alive to roast there. The familiar stench of roasting human flesh filled the area, and the vain screams of the leaders as they roasted were to me most eloquent expressions of the rage and pain they must have felt.

The brigands laughed and pointed at their roasting leaders, and they pitched more wood on the bonfire to be sure the leaders would be entirely consumed by the flames. One brigand then marched to the bonfire and raised a firebrand from the fire. He yelled a few words in a strange language and hurled the flaming torch into the wooden building. The building smoked a while and burst into flames. While the brigands continued to have their fun, we slipped back into the forest to get our hearties to work retrieving what had been the brigands' treasure.

In groups of ten, our men picked up the loot from under the tree roots. The Captain and I also hoisted two sacks each, and we all made our way back to the main trail out of the forest. We hastened along the dark path as best we could so that we could return to the landing of the port before first light. We stowed the treasure in the waiting whaleboats and rowed the boats and men back to our ships, where hearties hauled the bags on board in nets let over the side and took them to the Captains' cabins. By sunrise, our work was completed. We rewarded everyone who had participated in transporting the treasure with rum and rest for the rest of the day. The next morning we weighed our anchors and accompanied the dhow back to the sheikdom, as we had contracted to do.

When we arrived safely at our usual anchorage off the sheikdom, Captain Morgan and Alia went immediately ashore and visited the house of pleasure. There they were informed by the female consort of the sheik that the sheik had had a fit about the high price he was paying for protection. The potentate wanted to terminate the whole deal and take his chances on the shipments. He also planned to banish the Sweet Cutlass and the Night Lightning from his sheikdom since he felt he had been snookered and betrayed.

Captain Morgan, having anticipated the mercurial temperament of the sheik, asked the female consort whether she could arrange for him to present the sheik with gifts that he had brought back from his last venture. To grease the way forward, Alia handed the greedy woman a bag full of gold coins as a personal gift to use as she liked. The woman said she would see what she could do at once. In the meantime, she invited Captain Morgan and Alia to enjoy the pleasures of her house.

When the woman returned, she said that the sheik would entertain Captain Morgan the next day at noon in the space before his palace. There all his people would be assembled for the meeting. Captain Morgan thanked the woman for arranging things, and he rushed Alia down to the whaleboat to return to his ship to prepare. He had the coxswain swing by my ship and asked me to join him in his cabin on the Sweet Cutlass for an urgent meeting. I was perplexed by this hasty meeting, but I went as the Captain requested. He had already broken out a bottle of rum before I arrived, and he handed me one of the same. He was not in a good mood, but as we spoke his mood changed. Before the end of the meeting he was ebullient because we had evolved a plan.

At the outset of our meeting Captain Morgan put our situation succinctly.

"The sheik is planning to receive the gifts we brought and immediately to have me executed in public to demonstrate his power to his people and regain face with his female consort. She called him a fool for making a bad bargain with us foreign pirates. Our time doing security for this sheik has come to an end! How might we arrange a swift and honorable departure without losing our heads in the process?" I thought over the case as the Captain put it, and I had a few ideas for his consideration.

"First, the sheik has a lot of gold in his storehouse that needs liberation." This perked Captain Morgan up considerably.

"Second, while the sheik has no further need of our services, we certainly have no further need to be his servants. We've found another source of revenue that is less boring and more lucrative because we do not need to share it with a little potentate." The Captain brightened and took a swig of rum.

"Continue, Abe! I do like your line of thought."

"Third, we have enough time to arrange for the appropriate gift for the sheik to receive before his assembled people. We only need to borrow the sheik's own personal slave to help us convey the gift to his Highness's presence." At this, the Captain slapped the table and was about to rise to do a dance when I rapidly conjured a plan and asked him to tell me what flaws he could determine in it.

The Captain liked everything he heard, and with a wild gleam in his eyes, he agreed to proceed ashore immediately with Alia to do what I suggested.

That afternoon the female consort returned from the sheik's palace with the sheik's enormous personal slave, a man well over two meters tall with musculature like a man in the circus. We saw the slave to a private room in the house of pleasure and gave him rum that we commanded him to drink while he waited for our return.

That evening my hearties were busy all over the sheikdom. In the house of pleasure they beheaded, gutted and trussed the female consort of the sheik and placed the woman's head in a sack and her body in an empty tun, which they filled with rum and sealed with wax. The tun was attached to a cart that was drawn by one of the sheik's racing dromedaries outside the house of pleasure.

Along the shore, my hearties stove in the bottoms of all the sheik's dhows so that they could never be sailed again or easily repaired. At the storehouse, they overcame and killed all the sheik's armed guards. They beheaded them and impaled their dead bodies on long spears fashioned in the manner of Tamerlane, so that they stood on tiptoe with their heads lying beneath them all around the now-empty storehouse.

Finally, at dawn just before we left the sheikdom. Captain Morgan summoned the slave from the room where he had been drinking. He commanded the slave to carry a large, heavy sack in one hand and to lead the dromedary camel by a tether in his other hand to the open area in front of the sheik's palace. When he arrived there, the slave was to call forth his master in the loudest possible voice and to continue to call him forth until he came. Then the slave was to present the sack and the tether to his master and to say, "Compliments of Captain Morgan!" I rehearsed the slave so that he had the words down pat before he strode confidently forward to do as he had been ordered.

Captain Morgan and I then scoured the house of pleasure for all the rum that we could find and took them with us in our separate whaleboats to our ships. We laughed all the way out to the anchorage, and I thought I heard Captain Morgan's voice singing pirate songs while his hearties heaved ho and hauled up his anchor.

We had a good morning breeze to take us where we intended to go without much tacking. Soon we were sailing like innocent twin ships on a merchant adventure to the north in the Persian Gulf.

Looking landwards with my spyglass, I saw the tall slave with the camel and sack standing in the square in front of the sheik's palace. I plainly heard the slave's voice mimicking the words I had taught him.

He bellowed again and again, "Compliments of Captain Morgan!" I turned my spyglass to the Sweet Cutlass, where Benjamin was looking through Captain Morgan's spyglass at the figure of the slave in front of his master's palace. He lowered the glass and began to laugh. The parrot on his shoulder spread its wings and ruffled its feathers. It seemed to be laughing with him.

It was time to set the underway watch, so I called the order to the First Mate who relayed the order to the crew. The watch rotation went like clockwork, and soon we were sailing through the greenish, clear water as the sun rose higher in the eastern sky.

Fishing boats maneuvered to avoid the Night Lightning and the Sweet Cutlass as we unfurled our sails and increased speed.

I took station behind the Sweet Cutlass and ordered the helm to keep the ship in a line with the ship ahead. Then I relinquished the watch to the First Mate and went to my cabin.

My log entry for this last day in the sheikdom had promised to be a masterpiece of colorful prose, but all I wrote was, "Weighed anchor at dawn and sailed north in the Persian Gulf following the course of the Sweet Cutlass."

When I had completed my log entry and read it over, I wondered about how little a Captain's log told about a pirate's true adventures. A poetic pirate like Captain Morgan, who loved verses and songs, might have given his log entry a certain flourish.

The next time we enjoyed rum together, I decided to ask him what he wrote in his log this day so that I could compare that with my own record. For now, I just looked forward to getting back to our marauding in these target rich waters, where dreams of Arabia met the harsh realities of life.

Chapter Seven
Pirates of the Andamans

*O*n both of our pirate ships, the hearties sprawled on the weather decks in almost no clothing, sporting their battle scars and basking in the relentless sunshine while we sailed towards the fabled Andaman Islands east of India and north of the Strait of Malacca. The prevailing winds and currents were in our favor, and that meant we were swiftly putting India's Bay of Bengal behind us.

After our midnight raid on the gold bazaar high on the West Indian coast inland from the tiny smugglers' port, we thought we would probably not be welcome on those shores again. That was just as well, I thought, because pirates like us belong at sea.

Captain Morgan hatched the plan to steal the Indian gold, and as usual I executed his plan to perfection—with luck and the help of those of our hearties who formerly had been slaves. We had only just finished our circumnavigation off the Persian Gulf littoral, during which we captured, looted and sank three dozen prize vessels. We had then sailed down into the Arabian Sea through the wide bend of the Strait of Hormuz.

We had been careful before we made the strait to steer clear of the sheikdom, where we had left the sheik with the comely head and body of his concubine as a grisly farewell present.

Once we were well south of that bit of trouble and out of the Gulf, Captain Morgan called for a gam on the becalmed water to discuss how we might steal the mountain of gold that lay near a now-familiar small smugglers' port in India.

We plotted in our tethered whaleboats, drinking from bottles of un-watered rum. We were visible to both crews as we sat between Captain Morgan's ship, the Sweet Cutlass, and my ship, the Night Lightning. As was his habit, the Captain sang the pirates' song, "Fifteen Men on a Dead Man's Chest," and talked about the gold and then sang again about a beautiful woman with a strange disease, "The Lady Should Have Told Me but She's Dead." The more the Captain talked, the better his idea of getting the gold settled in my mind, though I did not like making a steady business of doing piracy on land.

In any event, I need not have worried as much as I did about our being attacked by troops during our approach to the bazaar's gold repository or during our taking of the treasure while we were there. I should, however, have worried about the ever-present brigands who appeared out of the forest on our way back to the port and tried to relieve us of our hard-won treasure of gold.

They made a lot of noise, but we discovered that brigands know nothing of fighting with cutlasses and knives as we pirates do. We cut the brigands all to pieces and then debated rifling their new hide, but we did not know their hide's precise location in the dense forest. We were already loaded down with gold and running late, so we returned with the treasure to our two waiting ships.

As for the scope of our pelf, it was beyond our wildest expectations. As our ships sailed south in tandem while hugging the Indian shore, we Captains counted the mounds of yellow coins and bars in our cabins.

Later we found a secret place to bury part of our treasure ashore in the pirate way near the tip of the continent. When our gold, pearls and jewels were securely underground with a fresh female corpse to guard them until we returned to exhume them, we turned our ships to a northerly heading, always remaining in sight of land while looking for prize ships offering booty on the bounding main.

I thought that the Captain would not miss his woman Alia since she had betrayed him with Benjamin. The Captain had cut off her head in a drunken rage when he found the two naked, with her moaning in ecstasy under the enormous black man. He did not threaten Benjamin for having had his way with the fickle woman, but he snatched Benjamin's beloved talking parrot from his shoulder, wrung its neck and plucked its colorful feathers. To show his displeasure, the Captain ordered Benjamin to roast the dressed bird for his supper.

The next day when we left the ship to bury our treasure, the Captain ordered Benjamin to carry Alia's head and body inland to be interred with the treasure. As Benjamin lowered her body parts into the hole, I thought the Captain would kill him on the spot. Instead, the Captain brought out a bag of colorful parrot feathers and scattered the feathers over the woman's cold, naked corpse and head. He laughed, drank rum and sang bawdy sailor songs—"She Surprised the Sailor with Her Charms" and "Bawdy Wench a Long Time Seeking" —while Benjamin filled in the hole and tamped it down. The former slave then carefully smoothed over the surface and covered it with cut foliage so that the place would not be found.

In a far better mood after exacting his vengeance, Captain Morgan returned to business matters and told me he had sailed in the Andamans as a young sailor. I believed him because he had experience of the whole world. He was impressed back then with the simple, happy lives that the Andaman islanders led. He said the young men traditionally set out on the sea to find adventure and possibly wives, since there were so few eligible women among them. They were not congenital pirates like the Malays, so they had no earthly ambitions. Captain Morgan called them "the lotus eaters" because they were as innocent as if they had been born in Eden and desired no possessions on account of their nomadic lives on the sea, where possessions would be a hindrance to their movements. Those nautical young men and boys, the Captain said, made excellent replacements for pirate hearties that had been lost in battle.

So Captain Morgan planned for us to shanghai a dozen or so strong, young men each to fill out our crews that had been thinned by our constant fighting. He had seen this done to good effect on the ship he had sailed when he was here last. He said that kidnapped Andaman islanders had adapted readily to the seagoing life, and they apparently never regretted sailing far from their home islands. They had no loyalty to any place or person, so they were natural pirates if only they could discover the right leadership.

When we reached the north islands, for a month we sailed around looking for men and boys we could lure onto our ships to augment our crews. For the promise of food or rum, or both, they flocked to ship aboard, and we had the fittest of those to choose from. To show we meant business, we made examples. When two potential recruits openly flaunted our offers, we slew them immediately and left their headless bodies as examples for the others.

We each selected twelve young men, and as we continued to scour the islands, we substituted a better new recruit for a worse among the former selectees. This did not faze our kidnapped males because they saw that merit was rewarded on pirate ships and that pirates ate well—far better than those who chose to make their home in the islands. The mates were in charge of the training of these new pirates, and individual hearties were identified as mentors to show the boys the ropes.

Before six weeks were over, our new watch standers were being schooled to watch the horizon for ships, to furl and unfurl sails and to do the thousand odd tasks that a pirate had to perform on the average day or night watch at sea. They each received a knife to use as a weapon, and we taught them to throw the knives and to use them in close combat. They lived with their new weapons and kept the knives razor sharp. A few we taught to use cutlasses and swords also. Before long, these men were going to need skills; without skills, the new men as pirates would surely die.

Our new sailors liked to be out on the weather decks in rain and shine. They were sure footed as they climbed the ropes and rigging and ran up and down the ladders extending from below decks to the weather decks. They quickly learned to drink rum and sing our pirate songs. Their needs were few, and they never complained of bad treatment when the hearties lost their tempers. One newbie named Hamad, who was raised as a devout Muslim, seemed to command respect among all his fellows, and he was a quick study. I ordered my First Mate to groom this lad as the future leader of the islanders for both ships. Hamad was a natural leader and excellent interpreter for his people, and he made friends with Benjamin, who as the natural leader of the former slaves was his counterpart.

No matter what else pirates do in their times between maritime battles, they prepare for what they must do in the dangerous trade of piracy. They practice throwing grapples, swinging through the rigging, sword fighting and knife fighting. These exercises are not games, but by encouraging the hearties to compete, I discovered that they could excel above their expectations.

So I encouraged completion among the Andaman islanders and among the former slaves as I did among the hearties.

Once a week for a bottle of rum I would have the crew throw knives and swords at targets, climb the rigging to the crow's nest, run from the weather decks down the hatches to the keel and back again, dive into the sea and swim around the ship three times without being eaten by ever-present sharks. The winner of each event received a long pull at a bottle of rum. The crew would vote the best overall performer, and he would claim a whole bottle of rum as his reward.

Captain Morgan did the same among his crew, and once a month we practiced our skills by conducting boarding exercises from one ship to the other. Captain Morgan also liked to swap the crews so that half of his came to my ship for a week while at the same time half of mine went aboard his. We did this to give our hearties a sense of comradeship across both ships.

We used our time in the north Andamans to bring our crews together and to overcome the petty differences that sometimes arose when the pressures of sailing soared, while at the same time the experience levels vastly differed among the crew members. The old hands were used to the changes wrought by bringing new crew aboard, but the former slaves were frustrated if the islanders did not respond perfectly the first time when ordered to do a task and every time thereafter.

I kept reminding the mates and the hearties that not long from now we would be up against bloodthirsty opponents like the Malay pirates who knew nothing about mercy. My hounding sounded extreme to the crew until we had our first introduction to the fierce south islanders.

The north islanders knew the south islanders as a different race. Where in the north everything was assumed to be shared by everyone, in the south the islanders fought for what they individually owned and captured whatever they could from others. I frankly liked the fighting spirit of the southerners, and I was bewildered by the insouciance of the northerners about treasure.

When we were anchored off the southern islands, the inhabitants would swim out to our ships and climb aboard any way they could. They would steal things and leap into the sea. So I offered a bounty to my crew for stopping the marauders, dead or alive.

Hamad took this to mean that the southerners should be killed rather than captured. So the north islanders of my crew began to repulse the south island boarders, and often when a south islander managed to get aboard and steal something, he met with swift justice in the form of a thrown knife in the back or a throat slit ear to ear.

When Hamad brought me a living south islander who had been trussed, I asked him what he thought should be done with the captive. Hamad did not answer in words but drew his razor-sharp knife and slashed his captive's throat. He then threw the body off the Night Lightning into the water while his fellow north islanders applauded him. From that day, I was sure that the new recruits could do what was necessary for successful piracy.

As we sailed from island to island in the south of the Andamans, we became aware of the large number and great variety of creatures that populated the land and waters of the region. Marked was the contrast of the north and south islands. Where in the north a few shells or native fruits were bartered, in the south the natives looked for gold and silver coins in all our exchanges. In the north, we never feared that the islanders were a threat to us, but in the south we saw good reason to be afraid of the denizens' perfidy.

One apparently mild mannered south islander grabbed one of the north islanders and drew his knife blade over the man's neck. He had seemed to be friendly right up until he committed his hostile act. Just after his crime Hamad's knife found the man's back. While the man died in agony, Hamad was inconsolable about the loss of one of his people. He told me that he would henceforth kill any south islander who came aboard my ship. He said this with such conviction that I knew he had been changed since his departure from his island—for the better from the pirate's point of view.

Our first taste of Malay pirate blood occurred while were still in the south Andamans. A pirate ship crowded with Malay pirates aspiring to loot the Night Lightning came head-to-head to ram us and board. As they maneuvered to come alongside, three score grappling hooks came flying through the air, and right afterwards the pirates swung like a myriad of monkeys towards our decks. The mates had readied the hearties for just this form of attack, and they moved to the sides with cutlasses and knives slashing every which way.

This show of resolve was new to the Malay pirates, yet they pressed their attack anyway with increasing vigor and savagery. I ordered my boarders to swing onto the Malay ship and fight their way below decks to scuttle the enemy ship.

Meanwhile, I ordered my mates to be alert for the Malays to do precisely the same thing when they swung aboard the Night Lightning.

In the melee I saw two of the new sailors and one of the former slaves cut down by the swarms of Malay pirates, and over the din of the shouting and fighting I heard the loud report of a cannon followed by the hollow sound of a tremendous explosion. I guessed correctly that my boarding party had reached the pirate ship's magazine and fired cannon filled with shot directly at the pirate's powder room, as they had been instructed and drilled to do. Immediately the Malay pirate ship began to list to starboard from taking on water below decks.

My hearties pressed against the Malays, forcing them either to return to their sinking ship at once or to die and be cast off the decks of the Night Lightning. Hamad and the remaining islanders ran amok at the Malays who were still on board our ship. They slashed in frenzy on all sides, and the Malays could not make a stand. To avoid being hacked to bits, the Malay pirates swung back on board their ship and feverishly began to cut all lines that led to our ship.

With the lines removed, the Night Lightning broke free and came about while putting distance between itself and the rival ship. Four of my hearties kept slashing at the pirates on the Malay ship, but they saw the way the battle was going, so they jumped into the shark-filled water and swam as fast as possible towards the Night Lightning where their mates had dropped lines over the sides so the swimmers could be hauled up onto our deck. Only one of the four swimmers was actually taken by a shark, and he died screaming. The other three swimmers made it to the lines and pulled themselves out of the water while my hearties on deck raised the lines to bring their comrades up to the deck's level and safety.

The Malay pirate ship that had attacked us did not sink all at once. It slowly rolled onto its side and continued to take on water yet stayed afloat a while. The remnants of the pirate force aboard her saw the feeding frenzy of the sharks in the water, and they knew that soon they would become the fishes' dinner. Some jumped into the water holding onto planks and other flotsam from their vessel, but their legs and arms were easy targets for the massive sharks that snapped at anything that moved or hung down into the water.

I offered no quarter to that vicious Malay pirate crew. In fact, I mused that if they had remained aboard my ship and we had taken them captive, they would now be walking a plank and falling into the same fish feed that they were soon going to experience. When the Malay pirate ship finally did sink, all the remaining pirates thrashed in the water until one by one they were taken under the surface by hungry predators. Finally the sea was entirely clear of all bodies and body parts. Everything indicating that a raging battle had taken place was reduced to a stream of bubbles that rose to the surface from the submerged and slowly sinking pirate vessel.

I asked the mates to muster the crew before the mast and report. We had lost six men, including two islanders, one former slave and the hearty who had been eaten by the shark. Three hearties had also been wounded, one so seriously that I gave him the coup de grace myself and ordered my hearties to add his body to the watery feast with the mantra, "More for the rest of us." I saw that the other two wounded had their flesh wounds bound with cloth tourniquets. I ordered a rum ration for all hands for a job well done: the crew had gained good experience fighting the Malay pirates together, but ours was a costly lesson. I vowed that we would suffer fewer casualties the next time around.

While the Night Lightning had fought one Malay pirate ship, the Sweet Cutlass had fought another just like it. They also slew all the pirates, but instead of sinking the vessel, they towed it while the Captain's crew raised the ship's treasure and valuables from its hold. The Sweet Lightning had lost seven men as the Night Lightning had done, and four of those had been among our former slaves. When we held our gam to assess the damage and decide what to do next, Captain Morgan said that we should ship aboard replacements to bring our crews to complement before we headed south through the Strait of Malacca to confront the rest of the Malay pirates on the sea lane and in their lairs along the Malay coast. Since we had a third ship now, the Captain suggested that we use it as both a training vessel in the short term and a lure in the long term.

We sailed north and visited the Andaman Islands, to the east instead of the west this time. Hamad was our recruiter because he spoke the islands' citizen's languages and could tell personal tales of his recent acts of bravado and daring while fighting against the ruthless Malay pirates. With his credibility among his people, we had no trouble adding fifty young men to our stable in one week.

Captain Morgan wanted not fifty, but one hundred prime recruits, and he wanted to cull out the weak and unfit early. He told me that we should bring aboard at least two hundred men and by testing and training work the number down to one hundred.

So we sailed from island to island for three months, growing our pool of north islanders as recruits and swapping out the better for the worse. We kept the recruits aboard the Malay pirate ship rather than the Sweet Cutlass and the Night Lightning.

Our Third Mates were put in charge of training, and the two alternated as Captain of the training vessel, which we renamed the Black Lagoon. That gave them experience of command at sea that they could not have obtained in any other way. It also created a third entity in our cabal, but we did not foresee the trouble that portended at the time.

Our three ships made a handsome sight when with full sail they raced and maneuvered around the Andaman Islands. Each day we all practiced closing and boarding, swordsmanship and knife handling, swimming and grappling and seamanship.

At one point we had two hundred and fifty able bodied recruits, and through attrition they became one hundred and twenty-five, and then one hundred. Only three men were killed during our training exercises. Carelessness and incompetence were the causes of two deaths, and an argument of one recruit with Hamad caused the other.

Hamad made his leadership over his people clear by slitting the throat of the would-be competitor before a direct challenge to his authority could be raised. After that incident, no one else ever tried to challenge Hamad's authority.

Captain Morgan placed his own First Mate in charge of the Black Lagoon when it was time to move south towards the Strait of Malacca. Fifty of the best, hand-picked recruits were integrated as two equal groups into the crews of the Sweet Cutlass and the Night Lightning. Captain Morgan stationed Benjamin on the Black Lagoon to serve as a kind of second in command and master at arms.

As I look back on this choice, I discerned the Captain's malice aforethought. What better way to achieve his revenge on Benjamin for sleeping with Alia than to send him on an impossible mission against bloodthirsty Malay pirates with a green crew?

The mission of the Black Lagoon was to serve as a lure for pirates in the Strait. They were to fly the French flag, unfurl maximum sail and speed well ahead of our other two ships, with her crew sunning themselves on the weather decks and appearing to have no real defenses against predators. When the Malay pirates tried to board her, the crew would bring their weapons from hiding and return the favor of the pirates by taking the attacking ship captive.

Captain Morgan and I decided we would lend a hand if necessary, but otherwise we would let the chips fall where they might.

We thought it was a good plan at the time. What we had envisioned was one attacking pirate ship, but when the Malay pirates attacked with three ships it was clear that all our forces had to mass to repel them. Two of the pirate vessels boarded the Black Lagoon to port and starboard simultaneously, while the third rammed her astern and boarded her from there.

The four ships were in minutes bound by lines with grappling hooks so that all four decks featured a melee of killing with men swinging from ship to ship.

Captain Morgan and I struck our false French colors and raised the Jolly Roger. We came outboard of the knot of four ships on either side and fired our cannon at close range to disable the mainmasts of all three pirate vessels and do as much damage to the structure of those ships at and below the waterline. We boarded from port and starboard with grappling hooks and lines fusing our ships with the others.

Now the Malay pirates fought us at the center on the Black Lagoon, where the casualties were many and across the decks of all the other ships. Since the Malays could not escape, they fought desperately, for they were without hope. We saw the meaning of the word "amok" for the enemy fought in desperation wildly and without discrimination.

I sent my Second Mate with a small party to scuttle the pirate ship next to the Night Lightning and simultaneously sent my Third Mate with another small party to scuttle the pirate ship that lay astern of the Black Lagoon.

Captain Morgan, seeing that the crew of the Black Lagoon was beleaguered and had been decimated by the fighting, sent most of his hearties into the thick of the fight, keeping only a few on board to defend the Sweet Cutlass.

I saw an opportunity to kill the three pirate Captains and seized it. I brandished my cutlass, grabbed a stray line and swung aboard the adjacent ship in the area of the helm, where I beheaded the Malay Captain. I then hewed left and right through the enemy until I saw a way to jump aboard the stern of the Black Lagoon and immediately jump to the focsle of the pirate ship at her stern. I had a long way to cut and slash through Malay pirates to reach the helm area, and I picked up a pirate's cutlass in my free hand so I could slash with two weapons at once as I proceeded.

At my side suddenly was Benjamin with two cutlasses in his hands. Like a two man killing machine, we lopped hands and heads all the way to the helm. There I let Benjamin have the honor of beheading the enemy Captain and slaying those who tried to defend him.

Meanwhile, I made my way back to the Black Lagoon and swung over to the pirate ship that lay next to the Sweet Cutlass. There by the helm I saw the Malay Captain shouting orders vainly to his dwindling crew. He did not see me come alongside him until it was much too late for him to react successfully, and as he raised his sword to strike me, I hewed his neck and his legs simultaneously so his head, torso and legs fell separately onto the deck with his useless sword all at the same time.

Now that the Malay pirates were without leadership on any of their ships, it was time for me to fight my way back to the Night Lightning. Two of the pirate ships were listing in the water because my hearties had scuttled them. When I reached my flying bridge, I yelled out for my hearties to cut all lines between the pirate ships and ours. I saw that my hearties had brought treasure out of the holds of the pirate ships they had scuttled. They were transferring the treasure to the Night Lightning before they shipped back aboard themselves. I understood and allowed the transfer but urged haste.

The denouement was balletic, I thought, as my hearties grabbed lines like dancers to swing back aboard and simultaneously cut all ties with the sinking pirate vessels. The remaining pirates had swung back to their sinking ships, learning only too late of their mistake. The Night Lightning drifted out to port from the two sinking pirate ships while the Black Lagoon drifted to starboard. Because of the blood in the water, a great many giant, hungry sharks had begun to gather for a feast, and the still-living Malay pirates learned to their horror that they would soon be food for those sharks.

I saw that on the other side of the Black Lagoon, the Sweet Cutlass was pulling off to starboard while the pirate ship to its port was listing badly and starting to sink. The hearties of the Black Lagoon were working frantically to cut all lines binding the sinking pirate ship to its starboard. Finally, she broke free from all the pirate ships sinking to her port, starboard and stern. The hearties aboard all three of our ships then scoured the decks for the bodies and limbs of dead Malay pirates and our own crews. As they cleared the decks and threw the human remains overboard, the fins of feeding sharks swirled in the blue and the water seemed to boil with feeding activity. The pirates on the sinking ships joined the feeding frenzy as food when their ships sank beneath them. Those who attempted in desperation to swim to one of our ships were torn apart by ravenous jaws and dragged down to the depths.

In a gam in the aftermath of the pirate raid, Captain Morgan and I reviewed the status of our crews. In our whaleboats we enjoyed some of the liquor that we had seized from the pirates. The Night Lightning had lost five hearties and the Sweet Cutlass had lost four. Of the crew of the Black Lagoon, twenty had been lost. All had gone to Davy Jones along with all hundred-odd Malay pirates.

Treasure seized from the three pirate vessels included gold and silver coins and bars, jewels, pearls, rich corals, ivory tusks, spices, bottles of wine and casks of liquor. The Captain opined that it had been a good day's work, but with far too many casualties. He said that we should try the same gambit tomorrow and hope that the Malay pirates came in a single ship only.

I told him that Benjamin had done valiant service this day, but the Captain only scowled in response and did not want to hear the details of Benjamin's service. We had lost none of our mates, he said, so we would not have to shift any of the crew. As for losing the north islanders, they were green and the survivors were now battle hardened. The lessons would make the survivors twice the men they were before the fight for their lives.

At first light the next day, the Black Lagoon sailed well in advance of our other two pirate ships, and it sported the French flag as before. A single Malay pirate vessel sped to intercept and board to starboard. The pirates were surprised that the apparently docile French ship turned out to be full of battle-hardened pirates who cut down all those who tried to board her.

The Black Lagoon quickly reversed roles with the pirate ship, and after killing the enemy pirates, they took time to rifle the stores of the pirate ship before scuttling her. After the pirate ship went down to Davy Jones, Captain Morgan and I sailed close enough to ask whether the Black Lagoon needed any assistance. Benjamin waved us off with his broad ivory smile and held aloft by its hair the severed head of the Malay pirate Captain.

The Black Lagoon then proceeded to unfurl its sails while the other two ships luffed sail to lend some distance between the vessels.

In the mid-afternoon a second Malay pirate ship intercepted the Black Lagoon and tried to board her, but it met with the same success as the prior pirate ship. This time some of the Malay pirates threw down their weapons and surrendered, but they were not held captive long before one by one they walked the plank into the shark-infested waters. When all her treasure and valuables had been transferred to the Black Lagoon, the pirate ship was scuttled and sank to Davy Jones.

Throughout that day, the Black Lagoon only lost five of her crew, three during the first attack and two during the second. She celebrated her victories late into the night with rum for all hands because tomorrow promised to be a very busy day.

The pirate coast was drawing nigh, and Captain Morgan's plan was to hug close to shore so that the Malay pirates would come out of their bays and attack in large numbers. Each ship was to be its own lure, surprise its attackers, seize the pirates' treasure and scuttle their ships.

The ruse worked like a charm. By evening, each ship had attracted three Malay pirate marauders. In the end all the enemy pirates had been killed, their treasure seized and their ships sunk. Two of the crew of the Black Lagoon had perished, but none had died on the Night Lightning or the Sweet Cutlass.

At our evening gam, I joked with Captain Morgan that we were doing the good work that the great powers should have undertaken to rid the sea of Malay pirates. The Captain responded by having a long pull of rum and singing some of his bawdy pirate songs, including two of his all-time favorites, "The Wench Wore the Pirate's Pantaloons" and "His Behind Arrears Before the Mast." I could tell the man was bored sick because the action in the Strait of Malacca so far had been unchallenging. He told me that he intended to pull out into the main and go after merchants instead of preying on the Malay pirates any longer. He needed the Night Lightning to provide over watch for him in case a warship tried to interrupt the fun.

I suggested that the Black Lagoon accompany us since it would otherwise be naked to attack by Malay pirates in great numbers.

In retrospect, it was prescient of the Captain to want me to watch his back, because he spied three rich Dutch merchants sailing in company and needed all three of our ships to pillage them.

Each ship intercepted one of the Dutchmen, and their sailing in company did no good for their security because none was a warship. We pirates had easy pickings. Each of our ships drew alongside her target and grappled aboard. All Dutch treasure, valuables, food, liquor and water were transferred to our ships before their ships' Captains were beheaded and their ship's crews were forced to walk the plank. We sank the three vessels rather than leaving them adrift in the Strait; with the three ships safe with Davy Jones, there would be no evidence of our piracy.

As evening fell, my lookout shouted that a warship was on the horizon, so we steered for shore and our fellow pirate ships followed us to an anchorage for the night.

Patrols of warships are mysterious to us pirates. I would prefer not to combat them because of their superior armor and fire power. They have a few things of great value, like small arms, gunpowder, shot, cannon, victuals, potable water and sometimes rum, but the sacrifice of crew for that kind of plunder is often not worth the bother. Running before the wind in flight is preferable to picking a fight with a warship, and only when you absolutely have to fight do you look for the best angle of attack and tactics that will mask your intent.

The next morning we observed that the warship we had remarked the night before was keeping station offshore from the location where we had chosen to anchor for the night. The warship's intention was clearly to board and inspect as many ships as it could while seeking pirates and treasure.

I did not like waiting for warships to come to me, so I set sail early with full sails and the French flag flying. I was trying to make it appear that mine was a pirate vessel trying to escape the one-ship blockade. The warship noted my tactic and set out to intercept. It fired cannon over the bow of the Night Lightning, so I luffed sail and waited for the ship to approach. My crew was all on the weather decks, trying to look innocent while concealing their weapons, all except for my gunnery hearties.

As the warship drew alongside and prepared to board, my cannon took out their main brace and the shot leveled the troops on the enemy's decks. My hearties uncovered their grapples with lines and hurled them so as to capture the warship. Over side swung my hearties as our cannon balls broke through the warship's hull and found the magazine with a dull explosion. The marines aboard the warship had been surprised by a hardened force like ours, but they were nonetheless formidable enemies because of their courage. Our desperation and innovation won over their heroism and drills.

My hearties slashed and stabbed their way across the warship's decks to her flying bridge, where they slew the Captain and bound the helm with line. They made their way below decks to haul up plunder while their comrades tidied up by killing all forces from the crow's nest to the keel. My hearties set up a high line for conveying the arms and pelf, and the transfer began in earnest when rum was discovered below.

I went aboard the warship for a time to see what was in the recently deceased Captain's cabin. I returned to the Night Lightning with papers that held much needed intelligence for me and gold that the Captain had hidden in a compartment. I also shipped aboard the warship's deceased Captain's private collection of fine vintage wines.

When I take a warship, I want no loose ends. I saw the last marines walk the plank and all that was left of the munitions, swords, knives, pistols, powder and shot transferred to my ship. I had my hearties fire the warship's own cannon so that her bottom would be breached.

All my crew returned to my ship before the warship keeled over and sank beneath the waves. I kept as a trophy the brass plate with the name of the warship that I took from the Captain's cabin, but that was the only remnant of that once proud warship after she went with her Captain and crew to see the bottom of the sea.

The papers that I found in the deceased Captain's cabin described a strategy for using many such warships as we had just sunk. They were supposed to be spaced all along the Malay coast to roust out the pirates in an operation that was meant to end the Malay piracies once and for all. This was bad news for pirates of all origins, including mine, and I had to get this vital intelligence to Captain Morgan as soon as possible.

When I returned to the anchorage that I had left earlier that day, I discovered only one ship at anchor, the Sweet Cutlass. I anchored nearby and called for a gam immediately. With Captain Morgan, I intended to discuss strategy for dealing with the situation of the warship blockade of the Malay coast.

The Captain told me that when I had set out to draw the warship away, the Black Lagoon had set out in the opposite direction to escape the blockade and go pirating on the main.

I told him that, under the circumstances, the Black Lagoon might now be in grave danger.

The Captain seemed to be preoccupied with his rum and his pirate songs, and he looked out on the Strait with a distracted expression as I told him the dimensions of the warship blockade.

When I had finished, the Captain said that we were likely to lose one or even two of our ships within the next two to three days. In all our days sailing together, I had never seen the man more melancholy.

He saw my concern and brightened up. He advised me to drink and eat heartily and to give rum rations to my hearties because tomorrow we might all die.

I told the Captain what else I had found on the warship I had sunk, and he nodded as if he did not think that mattered much in the long view. Then we returned to our respective ships. After brooding in my cabin for a time, I decided that I did not want to chance fate by just waiting for it to knock on my door, so I weighed anchor and sailed out into the Strait to see what had become of the Black Lagoon.

In fact, I discovered that the Black Lagoon had experienced a very good day of piracy and plunder. She had taken a French merchantman and transferred everything of value to its hold before scuttling the vessel. I had a gam with the now-Captain, who was of a mind to go on his own now that he had achieved a number of successes. I told him about the warship blockade, but he scoffed at the idea of that being a hindrance to his good piracy. When I asked him whether

Benjamin was of a similar opinion, the man gave me a fierce look but he agreed to let me speak with Benjamin for a few minutes. I therefore ordered my coxswain to steer for the Black Lagoon, and when we came alongside the Black Lagoon, I called Benjamin down into the whaleboat and explained the situation to him.

"Benjamin, warships are covering the entire Malay coast. They mean to root out pirates, and that will include us if we remain in this vicinity. Your Captain wants to break away from Captain Morgan and me and go pirate all on his own. That may or may not be a good idea, but it is certainly a dangerous idea at this time. We might be stronger if we stayed together than if we go alone. I know how you and Captain Morgan feel about each other after Alia's death, but I beseech you to come with me and let the Black Lagoon find its own path."

Calmly and respectfully, Benjamin said, "Captain Abe, you've always told me the truth, and I appreciate it. Captain Morgan and I will never be friends after what I did with Alia. I won't drive wedges between you and him, and I have allegiance to the Black Lagoon now, so I have to return to my Captain and crew. I'll see you when we meet Davy Jones together." I understood the man's point. I might have tried to force him to come with me, but that would not resolve his fundamental issues. Besides, he was a free man now and entitled to go his own way.

That was the last I saw of Benjamin face-to-face, an honorable pirate to the end. After we had conferred, I ordered my coxswain to return our whaleboat to the Night Lightning.

Once on board I immediately set sail for the shoreline, where I wanted to talk more strategy with Captain Morgan now that I had learned that the Black Lagoon had decided to strike out on its own. That evening in a gam by torchlight, the

Captain clenched his fists, raged and fumed, but he knew that nothing could be done now to remedy the situation with the Black Lagoon. In a very black humor, the Captain drank rum and sang dark pirate songs of death, ghosts, loss and loneliness, like "The Pirate's Ghost Danced for Davy Jones."

The Captain suddenly had enough of dejection. He shook his head, drank rum and, with a sparkle in his eyes, told me, "The only option for us is immediate clandestine flight to the South China Sea. I'm setting sail this very night, and I advise you to follow me."

I understood his logic and decided to follow his lead. We agreed to use Dutch flags as our cover, and by dawn we were pretending to be two Dutch merchants sailing in company in the middle of the Strait, both heading slowly on the usual commercial passage to the South China Sea.

As it happened, our course intersected that of the Black Lagoon, which was being boarded by marines from a warship that had found her suspicious. A second warship stood off covering the first, making rescue not only risky but also nearly impossible. We had the option to try to save the Black Lagoon, but we no longer owed the ship anything. We decided though as with a single mind to interpose.

The Sweet Cutlass headed straight to intercept the warship that was conducting over watch.

The Night Lightning headed to intercept the warship that was now boarding the Black Lagoon. We took the warships completely by surprise since they considered no opposition was likely or even possible.

As we approached, we hauled down our false colors and raised the Jolly Roger. We saw that our approach heartened our comrades on the Black Lagoon. They began to fight fiercely and loosed their cannon in a series of volleys as the boarders fled from her decks to defend against our oncoming vessels.

The Sweet Cutlass rammed the warship that was her target, and she came athwart ship and let forth a volley from her cannon that leveled the troops standing on her decks and took down her main brace.

The Night Lightning turned hard right and brought all her cannon to bear on the warship that was tightly coupled with the Black Lagoon. Withering volley followed withering volley, and the above-decks personnel fell while the masts split and shattered with splinters flying all over her decks. Another volley with balls aimed at the waterline breached the warship so badly that she began to list in a direction away from the Black Lagoon, whose crew cut all lines for fear of being pulled to the bottom as she sank.

Captain Morgan was not going to let this exercise be profitless, so he closed on his target and boarded her, with grappling hooks and lines flying and his hearties flying even before she made fast to her prey. The slaughter began immediately, and it did not cease until all the marines aboard were dead and sloughed off board to become shark meat. When all men were dead on their prey vessel, the hearties quickly made off with all things of value from the warship's armory to the hold of the Sweet Cutlass. The Captain's First Mate went to the cabin of the warship's Captain and came away with the gold the now deceased Captain had sequestered there. All the warship's stores were high lined to the Sweet Cutlass, and when this had been accomplished, Captain Morgan ordered the warship to be scuttled.

Meanwhile on the Night Lightning, I saw that the warship had rigged the Black Lagoon to be breached by her own cannon and sunk. There was nothing I could do to prevent the outcome. A tremendous explosion rent the ship in twain, and she sank at once with all hands. This was an affront to us pirates that I could not tolerate, so I ordered our cannon to fire unrelenting until no trace of the offending warship remained on the surface.

There was no sense searching for survivors of either vessel because the sharks feasted on all who hit the water from both the warship and the Black Lagoon. Thus I never saw the bodies of the Captain or of Benjamin. Unlike Captain Morgan, I did not have the sweet profit from the venture of destroying the warship that had sunk the Black Lagoon. I had only had the satisfaction of sweet revenge. My hearties told the mates that they were gratified that we had taken our revenge as they had comradeship with the members of the crew of our sister pirate ship.

When it was clear that the encounter with the warships had been resolved in our favor, the Sweet Cutlass and the Night Lightning hauled down the Jolly Rogers and hoisted false Dutch flags again. As if nothing extraordinary had happened beforehand, we sailed forth into the South China Sea, passing vessels sporting many different flags that were coursing both ways in the busy seaway that was the southern entry to and exit from the Strait of Malacca.

After we had sailed through the Strait, I followed Captain Morgan's lead as he steered a course along the eastern rim of land that marked the boundary of the Asian landmass. We began to see in these crowded waters junks of all sizes that in hundreds pursued fish and small cargo vessels that carried freight from port to port along the coast and then to mysterious China, hermit-like Korea and martial Japan. We knew that the pirates of the Philippines were active farther north, but for now we had no competition in our piratical trade. Therefore we began to pick our targets carefully and continue to do what we had always done.

We found that Dutch merchants and English were the richest to be plundered, but American and English were good targets also. So we came alongside and boarded almost four dozen vessels in the course of five weeks, and we took on gold and silver, jewels and pearls, silk fabrics and exotic minerals like jade and jadeite.

Until we reached the Philippines we brooked no opposition, and we pleasured ourselves by sending many vessels to see Davy Jones with all their crews. Sometimes we anchored off islands that were nothing more than seamounts, and sometimes we luffed sail to ride out typhoons and monsoon rains in the open sea. Once we saw the clouds turn golden by agency of a fine dust that blew out from China's vastness over the sea. We anchored off lands whose rivers emptied into the South and East China Seas, and there we let the hearties spend some time ashore buying women and trinkets while we took on water and provisions.

We had come a long way from the Persian Gulf, but we were still in sight of Asia. Captain Morgan and I considered what we should do in these waters, and we decided to plunder the ships that were heading to, or returning from China, Korea and Japan. Our expectations were fairly certain. We thought that those merchant ships that were inbound would be carrying gold and silver mainly and that those that were outbound would be carrying the goods of East Asia.

It turned out that the cargos were mixed. The best we harvested were warships because they carried gold and rum. There was, of course, a limit to what we could do with warships because nations under threat could band together against a common enemy. That is why our time in East Asia was limited.

So before five months had passed, at a gam off northern Japan, Captain Morgan and I began to consider what we would do next. He had been in these waters long before, but not much had changed in the interim. He suggested that we should provision ourselves well and then follow the trade routes across the vast Pacific towards the Americas, taking prizes as we went, and then follow the coast to Tierra del Fuego and sail around Cape Horn. That sounded fine to me.

I frankly liked the exotic East, but I knew that the pirate spirit in me would win out against my healthy but unprofitable curiosity.

Besides, I had found a beautiful and daring young girl named Xiaohong at a Chinese port we had visited. She had decided to join me in my cabin and explore the world with me. My cabin boy had long since grown into a man who needed to join the hearties to grow in the trade. So he was now on watch in the crow's nest, and gentle Xiaohong was in my bed.

Captain Morgan liked her so much he wrote a pirate song about her, "Red Port and Red Lady a Pirate's Love Affair." That was about the simplest summary of my trip to China, and the woman, the farthest thing from a curse upon my vessel, turned out to be worth her weight in gold.

Chapter Eight
Pirates of
Tierra del Fuego

The winds were very cold, and the sea state threatened all but the most stalwart of sailors and, of course, us pirates. Of all the passages of the world, Cape Horn was the most unforgiving, and it is impassable three to four months a year.

Two great oceans, the Atlantic and Pacific, come together there like the clapping of giant, watery hands, and large ships have been known to capsize and sink in less than five minutes with all hands lost. Even sailors lucky enough to be left on the gelid water's surface would die of the cold in ten or fifteen minutes, their only consolation being the comatose state they would reach after the first five minutes overboard.

The shores of the land called Tierra del Fuego were littered with the flotsam and jetsam of centuries of shipwrecks, and in between raids on the main, I sent my hearties scavenging. You never knew what useful things might be found among the jumbled remains of those hundreds of lost ships.

We had been hunting for merchants in those treacherous waters, sometimes sailing to the Atlantic side to catch a ship as she tried to get her bearings after passing around the Horn, but mostly we worked the west side of the Cape where ships, having passed the most dangerous trials, would drop their guard and become easy pickings.

We had sailed northwest out of the East China Sea when the Japanese warships made things difficult for pirates off their island shores. We finessed Korea because little of value went into or out of that hermit kingdom. Captain Morgan's grand plan was for us to sail around the great Pacific Ocean until we reached Cape Horn, where we would never lack for prizes if we could stand the elements.

It was a good thing we had the company of my woman Xiaohong, who now shared my bed in the Captain's cabin, because she was the scion of a nautical Chinese merchant family and therefore knew how to dress for sailing in the frigid northernmost and southernmost climes. She warned us to sail first to the northern strait between the two great continents of Asia and America, where she advised us to gather the warm skins and garments that we would use whenever we reached Cape Horn.

So we had sailed into the land of ice, sish, slush and snow, and we traded with the Eskimos for huge mounds of their skins and hides. With those raw materials Xiaohong fashioned me, herself, and each of my hearties on the Night Lightning, a warm suit of clothes that made Captain Morgan's crew jealous. Xiaohong then made cold weather garments for the Captain and all the other pirates of the Sweet Cutlass as well.

We wore those garments as long as we sailed in the Arctic waters, and when we boarded merchantmen who dared to sail those waters, we looked like Eskimos with our cutlasses and grappling hooks. Our captives were freezing and their teeth were chattering. Their vessels hung with ice. They put up no resistance, and only when they walked the plank into the green, icy waters did they realize the meaning of surrender.

Our time in the Arctic was excellent training, and we learned how to deal with chilblains and frostbite. Captain Morgan liked to shake out his long icy hair and his icy mustache and beard, and he would laugh for the fun of the experience and drink his rum. He took aboard his ship an Eskimo woman who had lost her husband on a walrus hunt.

Eida was her name, and she knew how to make meals from the fatty creatures of the region. She and Xiaohong became famous friends, and they shared Xiaohong's clothing when we sailed through milder climes as we headed south along the western coast of the Americas. When they worked side by side, I could tell the women apart, but at a distance and wearing the same clothing, they appeared to be identical twins. They both worked constantly to make us Captains' happy, and they were cheerful and sometimes playful with the hearties, who always treated them with respect.

Before we headed south, in addition to fresh water we took aboard barrels of whale meat, walrus meat and ivory, tuns of rendered whale oil, slabs of dried fish, skins of Arctic foxes and hares, three huge chests of old, blue Russian trading beads and twelve kayaks with oars—six kayaks for each ship.

We followed the old Russian trading route along the western shore, and we anchored out of Indian villages to trade, hunt and take on our usual provisions.

Captain Morgan received gifts when he went ashore, including a totem pole that he fastened to the mainmast of the

Sweet Cutlass so that its many faces looked him in the eye when he was in the area of the helm.

We did not meet any Russian traders as we passed through those waters, and we were well south of the farthest reach of the Russians when we began to encounter large Spanish merchant vessels, many of which became our prizes.

By then we had shed and stowed our Eskimo clothes and once again paraded around the decks in our pirates' rags. The warm sun felt better and better as we approached the Equator, and the hearties grew brown and orange on the weather decks.

Xiaohong and Eida wore fewer and fewer garments also, and they lifted the spirits of the hearties by sunning themselves where everyone could see them. Seeing how the Captain reacted when Alia slept with Benjamin, I was pleasantly surprised by his approval of the women's behavior.

"It does no harm to give the crew a glimpse of our rewards as Captains, Abe—as long as they don't try to sample our ladies' charms!" He laughed deep and long when he said this while his eyes noticed how every man on board admired the view.

We knew that we would not see much by way of silver and gold as we transited towards Tierra del Fuego, since the days of the Sixteenth-Century Spanish galleons with their loads of fabled yellow and white metal cargo had largely passed. Regardless of their cargo, any Spanish ship we saw caught our fancy. We did like the tuns of Spanish wines, and liquors that we took from the holds of some of those Spanish merchants.

Wherever the Spanish had sailed, they planted trees, shrubs and crops that could be harvested by later Spanish mariners and others also. Where we found them, we harvested those same Spanish-planted fruits and vegetables and included them in our diet.

Captain Morgan liked to squeeze oranges, lemons, limes and grapefruits into his rum and into red Spanish wines. Sometimes he would eat an orange or a lemon whole with peel, seeds, pith and all because he thought oranges and such were healthy. He encouraged his hearties to eat them, and some ate them with rum.

As we passed the Equator and the midday and early afternoon sun pounded the sea like a hammer does on an anvil, Captain Morgan would lounge under a canvas parasol on his flying bridge and sing his pirate songs and toast his hearties.

I could hear him from my deck as I watched Xiaohong comb out her beautiful black hair with a cunning comb she had brought with her from China. She sang her own songs, and sometimes she taught me what they meant. Her family had been pirates, and her songs told of her family's exploits in the East China Sea. One haunting song told of a woman who had drowned at the mouth of a great river called the Yangtze where it met the sea. The drowned woman's ghost haunted the intersection, where it waited for the man who had betrayed her and left her a spinster without hope of a child. When Xiaohong sang that song, the salt tears streamed down her face, but she would not tell me why she was crying.

We passed down the coast and heard tales on shore of other voyagers who had come from far to the west in the time of the native peoples' ancestors. Since we were not Spanish, we were a novelty, but the people, particularly their priests, were suspicious of us.

One Holy Father asked Captain Morgan in his cups whether he was a pirate. The Captain told him that he was a pirate when the mood struck him to be one, and he asked the

Father whether he had any objection to that. The Father unfortunately began to lecture the Captain about changing his ways and renouncing his chosen vocation. Captain Morgan listened intently to the Father, and then he drew out a pouch with a string around it and placed it on the table.

He asked the priest what he would do with twenty gold coins if he had them. The priest answered that he would use the money to build a new chapel to honor the Lord. The Captain then opened his pouch and poured twenty gold coins on the table. He said the priest could take the coins as his offering and build his chapel and give any residuum to the poor.

The priest was now in a quandary because if he took up the gold coins, he was taking stolen money from an acknowledged pirate, but if he did not take up the gold coins, he would not be able to build his chapel or feed the poor.

Captain Morgan laughed heartily and began to recite the Nunc Dimmitis. He then recited the Ave Maria and Pater Noster.

I who was there beside him had never heard the Captain utter as much as a word of Latin before. I had never suspected him of knowing anything about the papist religion or any other religion for that matter.

When Captain Morgan was done with his recitations, he stood up from the table and departed the establishment, leaving the gold coins and his empty pouch lying on the table. I followed him out the door.

When we reached the village square, the Captain burst out laughing and slapped me on the back. He drew a bottle of rum from his pocket and offered me a swig. Then he took a long draught, smacked his lips, and told me that he once had studied to be a priest. He laughed again, and he said the trouble was that he liked women more than he liked the men who did not like women. Then he became meditative and we walked back to our whaleboats by the shore in silence.

I do not doubt the Captain's word that he once considered being a priest. I thought no less of him for admitting the fact. I marveled that I was still learning things about this complex man despite all the time we had spent together roaming the world as pirates.

The Captain had heard of a place where gold ore was mined. The ore was refined, and the refined gold was shipped to Spain. Spanish merchant ships came to pick up the gold in bars and returned an equal amount in weight of gold coins. Captain Morgan wanted to assess whether it was true that the gold in bars was of equivalent weight to the gold in coins. The only way to do that, he said, was to obtain both and do the comparison.

He hatched a plan by which he would stand off the port where the Spanish merchant anchored. While I went ashore with my hearties to liberate the gold coins that had been traded for the gold bars, Captain Morgan would liberate the gold bars from the Spanish merchant ship. We would meet off the coast a few miles to do the comparison.

When we reached the small port, we both anchored out and I took my whaleboat to the shore to reconnoiter. A fort loomed on a hillside with soldiers patrolling its ramparts. Soldiers guarded a store house at the center of the village square. The problem with the Captain's plan was clear to me; it would be impossible to steal the gold coins on shore without undue risk to my hearties.

I decided to look into matters further, and I discovered from the village prostitute that the soldiers had not been paid in many months. They were expecting to be paid their arrears when the merchantman came the next day with the coins that were to be used for payment. The prostitute said that many soldiers owed her in arrears for her services, so I gave her two gold coins and told her that I would give her two more gold coins if she told me when and how the gold bars that would be traded for the coins would arrive.

She laughed heartily and told me that everyone in the village and the fort knew that the gold bars would come by carriage two hours before dawn on the road from the refinery. She said that many soldiers guarded the refinery and the store house, but only two guarded the gold bar shipment itself.

I gave her the additional two gold coins, departed the village and went back to my ship at anchor. I signaled to the Sweet Cutlass that I wanted a gam with Captain Morgan. At the gam, I explained the situation and outlined a revision to our plan.

That evening I went ashore in my whaleboat with five of my fiercest hearties with spades, and we walked out the road to the refinery. At a likely spot, just after a slight bend in the road with foliage that could hide us, we stopped to dig a wide, steep rut in the road. We rolled five large rocks to block the passage beyond that. We lit some hemp and brought out bottles of rum that we had brought to pass the time and waited. At this same time, Captain Morgan weighed anchor and sailed out in darkness to greet the Spanish merchantman that was to bring the gold coins to exchange for the gold bars from the refinery.

Three hours before dawn, I heard the report of cannon out over the main, and I suspected that the Spanish merchant had been cheerily greeted by the Sweet Cutlass.

When the carriage with the gold bars came an hour later, it fell into the rut the hearties had dug and broke its front wheels while the horses pulling the carriage reared in confusion.

My hearties charged the two soldiers that were guarding the treasure. The whole business was done in two minutes. We harvested the gold bars and used the untethered horses to bear them to the landing, where we loaded the bars into the whale boat and departed just before dawn. As we had planned, the Night Lightning had weighed anchor and was waiting for our arrival to depart the anchorage.

Dawn came and no ships were visible in the anchorage. Three miles offshore, the Night Lightning and the Sweet Cutlass made a rendezvous and a gam.

Captain Morgan was indignant at the gam. After carefully weighing the gold coins and gold bars, we discovered that the gold bars outweighed the gold coins by three to one. The exchange, we thought, had been utter piracy. Spain was making two hundred percent on its investment!

Our piracy was at least honest labor that required nothing from anyone except, of course, the gold. The Captain and I drank rum while we inveighed against the greed and deceit of the world powers, of which Spain was only one. Then the Captain began singing his pirate songs, and I knew it was time to return to our ships and unfurl our sails.

To be fair, we split the coins and bars down the middle, though I had argued that perhaps I should keep the bars and he the gold. He may have seemed drunk beyond reason, but Captain Morgan spotted the problem with that deal immediately and fell into a dark humor. As he rowed off with his share, the Captain sang a song that ran, "Pirates be good to fellow pirates, else 'Avast!'"

So we sailed south, and the weather became increasingly cold until we sighted a village that may have been the farthest habitation to the south before Tierra del Fuego. By then we were all wearing our Eskimo clothes again, and we were anxious to see how bountiful our new hunting grounds would be.

When we had anchored and gone ashore, we found the village was long deserted. We noted that livestock pens were still in good repair, and the buildings were in need of only minor alterations to be livable. We decided that the village was as good a habitation for pirates as we could hope for, so we brought the hearties ashore to fix things up. We named our village Hearties Village, and in no time it was shipshape.

Naturally, the best two dwellings in the village were reserved for Captain Morgan and me, and our two women were delighted to have arrived at a place on land that they could call their own. Xiaohong and Eida made homes out of their two houses, planting trees, bushes and flowering plants and setting up kitchens.

Dwellings were also identified and set aside for the First, Second and Third Mates from each ship, but those mates and their hearties preferred to remain at sea and live on board their ships rather than become comfortable ashore as landlubbers. Instead of occupying the dwellings, they made one of them into a tavern, and we provisioned it with casks of rum from floor to ceiling along one wall and casks of wine likewise along the opposite wall.

Across from the tavern's entryway was a wall that the hearties knocked down to form a large open hearth where a roaring fire raged all night long. Tables and chairs made the place a kind of mead hall for pirates, and we Captains as well as the crew drank and held forth there when we were ashore. Since the other dwellings were empty, we prudently made them storehouses for our pelf, and such was our success at piracy that it was not long before those storehouses were full to capacity. We eventually had to build new storehouses to accommodate our growing wealth.

Hearties Village was perfectly situated for piracy because the prevailing winds carried us right down to our prey running in both directions around Tierra del Fuego. After first transiting around Cape Horn, we became accustomed to the rip tides, currents and winds where the oceans collided. We also learned how we had to maneuver to our advantage so that we could plunder the merchants that we wanted and avoid the warships that would certainly come in due course.

I sailed down once to examine the ice continent that lay far to the south of the Cape, but I saw no advantage in spending time there. Huge flocks of penguins frolicked. They might serve as food if we ever had need of them. Sailing close to the eastern shore of the extreme south of the Americas for a half day's voyage, I saw no advantage for planting a village such as Hearties Village on the western side. We had done well with our choice of habitation, I thought at the time. If only we had animals to fill our empty pens, we would have lived in paradise.

We began a routine that worked like a properly wound clock. On average, each of our ships seized, plundered and sunk three or four merchants each week. Since we had created additional storehouse space on land, we offloaded our excess valuables and stores at the end of each week, regaled our hearties with rum in our warm tavern and set out again at the beginning of the new week to continue our work off the Cape. We took Spanish, Dutch, German, Italian, Portuguese, French, English and American ships.

I raised flag poles around the village to sport the colors of the nations whose ships we had captured and sunk. It was our game to find a prize with a flag we had not taken, but we soon found that most of our booty came from only a few nations' merchantmen.

The Asian trade and the Spanish colonial trade were the two main commercial enterprises that made the water off Cape Horn an important choke point in world commerce. Nations depended on the trade that crossed between the Atlantic and Pacific around Cape Horn.

Therefore, Captain Morgan estimated that it would take six to nine months before the big maritime trading interests would become wise to our piracy. He said that factors would report ships we had sunk as missing, and those who insured the ships' passages would have to pay for their lost cargos. In due course insurance rates would rise.

Consequently, important, moneyed people would start wondering why so many ships rounding Cape Horn were disappearing all of a sudden. Those people would want answers, and they had the power to influence governments. Warships would be sent to assess the threat of piracy.

Then, the Captain said, our game would have to change. I understood what the Captain said, but I could not hold his ideas with the same burning sense of conviction that he did. He told me that it would be unwise to let Xiaohong and Eida know about the transitory nature of our stay in Hearties Village. When retribution came, we would either have to fight and die in defense of what we had built or pack and flee beforehand and never look back.

I knew how the women felt about settling down for good. The Captain's decision made sense, but I knew they would be disappointed. All things considered, though, I do not like anyone's getting rooted in one place for long. Stability makes both men and women weak and vulnerable. It is better for us to move frequently and to struggle rather than lose our souls in complacency.

I have never believed in panic because I have seen what that does to men. It makes them craven cowards and breaks their will to survive. I did see the wisdom in porting some of our pelf from Hearties Village to a new location. So I decided to look again for a storehouse venue on the eastern side of the coast leading to Cape Horn.

I told Captain Morgan I would do a scouting mission for a week while he continued to plunder ships around the Cape. Accordingly, the Night Lightning proceeded north and east along the track I had already taken, but this time I was alert to nuances in the landscape that would permit us to hide our treasure and valuables at least temporarily. I sighted a river's mouth emptying into the Atlantic and figured that fresh water could be had there, so I anchored out and went ashore with a few men to scout the areas to the north and south of the river.

The general lie of the land was perfect for burying pirate treasure. I had an eerie feeling that other pirates had reconnoitered this place before, and someone had perhaps buried treasure here. I looked for likely landmarks and found an ancient tree. With two of my hearties I circled the area around that tree in an expanding spiral, looking for loose ground or the slight declivity that might mean a former burial. We found such a place thirty paces to the north of that tree, and I asked the hearties to lend a hand and dig. Six feet below the surface they hit solid wood, and they worked fast to uncover a skeleton over a chest. Unearthed, the chest revealed gold and silver coins, a pirate's hoard for certain. My hearties were glad to carry this unlooked-for treasure to our whaleboat and then to the Night Lightning.

Meanwhile I continued to look for other signs of pirate hoarding, and I found the hearties that had searched to the south of the river. They had found a stone with a crude marker near it in the form of an arrow. So we followed the direction of the marker and found a mild depression, which I ordered the hearties to investigate by digging a hole three feet wide and as deep as they could delve. The hearties quickly dug through scrabble and finally struck a skull with a chest below it. They unearthed the chest and saw the gold and silver treasure that was within it. They took it to the shore, and when the whaleboat returned, the coxswain rowed us all and the found treasure back to the Night Lightning. We had thus in a single landing uncovered two stores of pirate treasure worth a king's ransom.

I had to ask myself how it was that this treasure had become interred in this godforsaken place. The treasure must be the result of other continuous pirate ventures in the area surrounding Cape Horn. I began to think why the treasures had come to be buried where they were found, and I had a wild surmise. What if, I thought, pirates had inhabited Hearties Village just as we had, and they had seen the future clearly and decided to hide their treasure on the opposite side of the Cape? They must have done exactly what I did. Coming to the river, they hid their treasure to the north and the south in the usual pirates' way. They evidently had never returned to retrieve their wealth. But why? The only answer I could devise was that they were all killed. If they had found a congenial safe harbor in the village that we now called Hearties Village, they had been systematically exterminated or forced to flee without their treasure. It was more likely, I thought, that they had been exterminated. I now feared for Hearties Village, and as I set sail to return there, I began to devise a plan for our next steps. It would have been madness to continue as we had done for the last few months.

While I was finding pirates' hoards, Captain Morgan had experienced the pinnacle of piratical success in his ventures against rich merchants rounding Cape Horn. He had taken five ships in my absence, and he was feeling invincible when we had our gam outside the anchorage for Hearties Village.

"Captain, congratulations on your conquests since we parted last. While you were taking treasures from merchants, I was discovering pelf buried by pirates long since gone, a tremendous hoard of gold, silver and jewels, now ours." I told him over a bottle of rum what I had found on shore on the other side of the Cape. I explained what I had reasoned about why the gold and silver had been hidden and why the former villagers had disappeared. At first I did not think the Captain had heard me because he began to sing his usual pirate songs and took long draughts of the bottle of rum.

But he had moments of absolute clarity, and his eyes pierced me to the soul when he said, "I know that pirates preceded us. I know who they were and why they will never be returning."

Captain Morgan then launched into a horrific story of pirates who became too soft because they had discovered a good thing.

"They had taken women and done all the things that a landlubber does to guarantee the futurity of his women and children. They were discovered by troops of one of the nations whose ships they had plundered. In this case it was the English. The pirates were wiped out in a concerted attack. All their ships were sunk, and the English marched ashore to kill everyone: man, woman and child in their pirate village. If I stretch my brain, I could tell you which warships and which Captains had been involved because only a few competent Captains know how to eradicate entire pirate communities. It doesn't matter what was done in the past. For now the same is about to happen, and we have to make a plan."

"Captain, I formulated a plan while I returned from gathering the treasure on the other side of the Cape. The treasure I found dwarfs all we have amassed in the time since we arrived in this region." I told him my plan in detail.

The Captain seemed to like my plan, but he said, "Xiaohong and Eida will not like it, not one bit."

I now took a long draught of the rum and told Captain Morgan, "It's only a matter of a little time before we have to execute my plan."

"I agree, but I have a few modifications for our plan."

I listened with increasing interest because he seemed to have thought everything through beforehand. I was convinced when we had finished our gam that we had to act at once. We anchored our ships, and I went directly to Xiaohong and told her the situation.

"In short, we have to pack and depart right away. The alternative is slaughter. We would not stand a chance."

Xiaohong was not surprised. "My people always had to keep on the move. They never rested because they knew that their pursuers would never relent. So I'm ready to leave everything that we've built tomorrow."

I knew then that I loved her, and I told her, "Prepare and be ready to leave when the decision is made. In the meantime, gather what you treasure to take with her."

With tears welling up in her eyes, she hugged me close. "What I treasure most is you."

I met Captain Morgan in the tavern, and he told me that Eida had told him much the same thing that Xiaohong had told me. I suggested that we execute our plan as soon as possible. He was, as always, a step ahead of me. He had already prepared his hearties to transport half the treasure and valuables that we had amassed to the Sweet Cutlass, and he advised me to have my hearties transport the other half of our pelf to the Night Lightning. He said that we should leave the village exactly as we had first found it, so everything we had done had to be undone.

All this took another two weeks of hard labor involving the crews of both our pirate ships. Finally, the village was empty and as void of evidence of recent habitation as when we first came upon it, with our women living again aboard the ships and the village looking as deserted as it had been when we had arrived.

The one exception was the flags of many nations that hung from poles at the village's center and played in the winds. Liking what we saw, we weighed anchor and made headway as the sun rose that final day off Hearties Village. We were not leaving under the threat of immediate attack; instead, we were leaving on our terms, with our treasure and all our hearties alive and our women content to make the shift to other quarters.

As we rounded Cape Horn with our false Spanish colors flying, we passed a group of American warships that may have been sent to discover our whereabouts and destroy us, but we would never know the truth of that since we had already vanished from our haunts.

I was too wise to think that we had escaped just in the nick of time or any such rot. We had made a business decision that required our relocating. We had not waited to be evicted or to be threatened with extinction. Rather, we had taken what we had earned and departed. We were riding heavy in the water because we had loaded all our treasures, but we were still sea worthy.

We continued within visual range of the shore up the Americas, stopping to take on provisions and trade. Since we saw increasing signs of genuine Spanish vessels, we shifted to the false flags of the Netherlands. Neither off Portuguese Brazil, nor off Spanish Argentina, were we challenged as we sped north with full sails.

We reached the Caribbean Sea before we stopped worrying about pursuers. We were now too far away from Tierra del Fuego to be considered credible perpetrators of what had happened there. No one would suspect that the empty village had been used by us pirates. No one would check on the opposite side of the landmass to find the exhumed remains of the burial of treasure that had been removed.

Captain Morgan reasoned that Davy Jones himself would have to be subpoenaed to testify against us in a court of law, but Davy did not care who had sent vessels his way. He reveled in the mayhem on the high seas, as everything on the sea finally ended in his domain on the sea bottom below it, and Davy Jones' locker attested to his gains and the mariners' losses.

Captain Morgan did not believe in looking backwards. He was now again in prime hunting grounds that he knew — the Caribbean. He had been around the world again searching for better, but he had not found it.

I had to agree that we had seen the world together. Partly because of the Captain's former experience, partly because of our combined ingenuity and partly because of luck, we had survived our ordeal and returned to tell our tales.

The Captain's songs reflected what he had seen this time around. He sang of an Eskimo lady whose husband had not returned, but she had found a pirate who loved her better than her former mate. He sang of a fool who fell in love with a Chinese woman who knew he was a fool and would betray him. He sang lots of new songs that I'm sure he composed on his own. After all, he was a man of many talents, a genius poet, a genius pirate and a natural drunken rogue.

We buried treasure all around the Caribbean in the pirate way. Eida may have marked one such hoard, because she disappeared on the day Captain Morgan set out in his whaleboat to hide a large part of his treasure in Dominica. Xiaohong may have marked another because she disappeared the day I set out to bury a hoard of gold bars and coins in Haiti. That was what the hearties thought, and we did not contradict them.

As I look back over our escapades since we left the Andamans, I saw a broad continuity of our actions. Pirates are romantics, and our treasures are extensions of ourselves. I laugh when I think of leaving all those flags of all those nations at our village near Tierra del Fuego. If the flags survived, they would have tantalized the warriors who pursued us. What would they have learned from those flags? Perhaps they would have learned that pirates have a sense of humor. Perhaps they would have learned that pirates know when to fish and when to cut bait. Most likely, though, they would have learned nothing. In their single-minded pursuit of an unknowable enemy, they would have missed the point entirely. They would have arrived where we had enjoyed a few months of perfect piracy only to find that their prey had fled they knew not whither.

At a tavern in San Juan, Captain Morgan and I decided we would go our separate ways.

"I've taught you what you need to know to survive. I've circumnavigated the world with you, and we have nothing to teach each other anymore." His tone was earnest and resigned.

"Captain, it has been an honor and privilege working with you. I sincerely doubt I've learned all you can teach me. I must respect your wishes. Yet one day you may decide to go pirate again. On that day, think of me. We'll hoist the Jolly Roger together." I was disappointed and sincerely thought I had only learned a fraction of what this masterful pirate had to teach.

We drank rum, and he sang pirate songs. He stood on the table and brandished his sword. He railed at the host, and he called for the ladies to parade before him naked. Then he collapsed, and I asked two hearties to help me carry him to his whaleboat, where his coxswain was waiting to take him to the Sweet Cutlass.

What happened to Captain Morgan from that time forward, I do not know. I heard rumors of his having had many adventures in the Seven Seas. I heard that he went to Davy Jones and bested him for all his treasure. I heard that he had retired from the trade and gone to a place he had prepared for himself in Dominica, where he now lived with Eida, who was alive and well and entertaining whoever her now-husband wanted to bring home.

I thought that was the least likely of the possible outcomes, but it had the ring of truth. By my lights, at least, it had that tone, because my Xiaohong and I live well in Haiti in a spacious house with a view of the harbor.

She accommodated quickly and well to the new environment, and she loved the vegetation that luxuriates without her tending or care. She laughed when I told her I was going to give up being a pirate, and when I am sad she goads me by insinuating that I will fly the Jolly Roger again one day.

We have five children, who are the light of my life. I know where untold treasures hide around the world, and I could sail tomorrow to dig up whatever my family needs. I have a good life, and the past is forgotten because by now all my hearties have gone to Davy Jones or been hanged by landlubbers who have no earthly idea what piracy really means.

I compiled all of Captain Morgan's songs that I remember, and I want to have them properly published someday. I will not own them because he composed and sung them, but the pirate songs were not as much his property as they were the product of the rum, his fertile brain and the people and situations that they evoked.

I thought of Captain Morgan's women, and I wondered that all those various females could live with a pirate with such wildly varying moods. I thought of his numberless women on shore and how they served as his intelligencers and seers.

I thought of the man's vision and insight into human beings. He was a leader among outlaws, and his presence evoked allegiance. He won mine, surely. I felt the attraction of his personality, and it changed my life entirely. He was my mentor, my teacher, my brother and my friend. I would miss him if his memory were not always with me somehow. I sometimes fancy he will pop up in a whaleboat singing his songs with a bottle of rum at the ready and invite me down to talk of some new scheme for piracy.

The Sweet Cutlass, I am told, was sunk by a British warship that took out her mainmast and then volleyed a broadside at her waterline before scattering shot across all her decks, killing all aboard. Captain Morgan had long departed before that sinking ended a legacy. The Night Lightning, I am also told, was sunk by an American warship that boarded her, killed all the hearties aboard at the time and stole all her gold before scuttling her.

Both pirate vessels suffered ignobly at the end, but then a ship is only to be known by the spirit of the men who sail her. When Captain Morgan and I departed, those ships changed utterly. We changed too.

Now I am the entity I hated most when I was a pirate sailing the main, a landlubber. Xiaohong and the children like the change, but I know that if we had to set sail again, my wife would sail with me as she always has done in the past. We would set sail together without looking back and have whatever treasure we pleased from any corner of the world.

Author E. W. Farnsworth was born in California and now lives and writes in Arizona. E.W.'s collection of crime stories, *John Fulghum Mysteries*, and his romance/thriller, *Engaging Rachel*, were published by Zimbell House Publishing in 2015. His *John Fulghum Mysteries, Volume II*, will appear from Zimbell House in 2016.

Bitcoin Fandango, Farnsworth's picaresque novel about global intrigue in cryptocurrency enforcement, appeared from Greenman Arizona Press in 2015.

Along with Farnsworth's first collection of western stories, *Desert Blood, Red Blood*, 2015, Pro Se Productions will offer his techno-thriller spy stories, *The Secret Adventures of Agents Salamander and Crow* as a monthly Single-Shot series starting in 2016 and as a collection thereafter. His *Desert Sun,*

Red Blood, Volume II, and *Dead Cat Bounce,* an Inspector Allhoff mystery novel, are to be published in the near future.

E. W.'s collected science fiction stories will be published as *DarkFire at the Edge of Time* in England by Audio Arcadia Publishing in 2016.

Eighty-three of his short stories published during 2015 including many in Zimbell House Publishing anthologies. Some of E. W. Farnsworth's sci-fi stories and modern fables are available on line from Ether Books and Jotters United in the UK and fictuary.com in the US. Two of his earliest John Fulghum mysteries will be available on line in 2016 at IndelibleCHAOS in India.

E. W. is now working on an epic poem, *The Voyage of the Spaceship Arcturus,* about the future of humankind when humans, avatars and artificial intelligences must work together to instantiate a second Eden after the Chaos Wars bring an end to life on Earth.

Farnsworth also just completed a novel about Gypsy life in Europe during the Nazi era for Zimbell House Publishing.

For continuous updates on current and forthcoming works of E. W. Farnsworth, please see:

www.ewfarnsworth.com.

Reading Group Guide

1. Throughout their adventures, violence is a keystone to the pirates' way of life. Did you find their violent ways off-putting? Why or why not?

2. Despite their flaws, did you find any positive personality traits among the pirates (such as loyalty, teamwork, fairness, etc.)? If so, did these values help make the pirates more relatable or noble in your eyes?

3. Were you surprised by the pirates' dislike of slavery? What do you think this says about their moral code?

4. The pirates visited many different places throughout their travels. Which location was your favorite, and why?

5. What was your favorite scene in the book, and why did you choose this scene?

6. Abe clearly admires Captain Morgan. Do you think his admiration is warranted? At any point, did you feel that Abe may have surpassed Captain Morgan as a capable Captain?

7. How did you feel about Abe's decision to settle down at the end of the story? Were you surprised that he was willing to give up the pirate lifestyle?

8. Did you find the characters and their actions believable? Were there times you were surprised by the characters' actions or thought they should have behaved in a different way?

9. Captain Morgan and Benjamin both alienated one another through their actions. Did you side with one more than the other?

10. How did you react when Benjamin decided to leave Captain Morgan? Did you find his actions selfish or logical?

11. Captain Morgan's fate is ambiguous at the end of the story. What do you think happened to Captain Morgan?

12. Do you think Abe will return to sea one day, or will it be too difficult for him to leave the landlubber life?

A Note from the Publisher

Dear Reader,

Thank you for reading E. W. Farnsworth's novel, *Pirate Tales*. We feel the best way to show appreciation for an author is by leaving a review. You may do so on our website www.ZimbellHousePublishing.com, Goodreads.com, Amazon.com, Kindle.com, or Smashwords.com.